While You Were Gone

A Christmas Second Chance Romance

by Michelle Love

Published in United States by:

Michelle Love

© Copyright 2020 – Michelle Love

ISBN-13: 978-1-64808-014-2

ALL RIGHTS RESERVED. No part of this publication may be reproduced or transmitted in any form whatsoever, electronic, or mechanical, including photocopying, recording, or by any informational storage or retrieval system without express written, dated and signed permission from the author.

Table of Contents

Synopsis...1
Prolog 5
Chapter One 8
Chapter Two..16
Chapter Three 26
Chapter Four 36
Chapter Five 44
Chapter Six 53
Chapter Seven 65
Chapter Eight 73
Chapter Nine 82
Chapter Ten...90
Chapter Eleven 96
Chapter Twelve 103
Chapter Thirteen... 108
Chapter Fourteen 115
Chapter Fifteen 119
Chapter Sixteen 125
Chapter Seventeen 132
Chapter Eighteen 137
Chapter Nineteen 144
Chapter Twenty 152
Chapter Twenty-One 156
Chapter Twenty-Two... 167
Chapter Twenty-Three....................................... 174
Chapter Twenty-Four 182
While You Were Gone Extended Epilogue 186

Synopsis

Young Manhattan editor Maia's life falls apart two days before Christmas when her husband and daughter go missing. Desperate to find them, she is devastated when her husband's car is found next to a notorious suicide bridge with a note that simply reads "I'm sorry."

For the next five years, Maia struggles to come to terms with the tragic loss. Finally she begins her life over, moving across the country to Washington state and opening a local book shop on one of the islands in Elliott Bay.

She begins rebuilding her life, but when she meets enigmatic architect Atom Harcourt, they begin an erotic, passionate love affair, and Maia finally finds happiness.

Soon a series of troubling incidents lead Maia to believe someone is targeting her, and as the five-year anniversary of her family's disappearance looms, malevolent forces surround her, and she doesn't know who to trust.

Will Maia ever find the answers she is looking for? And who is the mysterious stranger lurking in the shadows… and is he a stranger at all?

This is a romantic suspense novel perfect for the holidays with no cliffhanger, plenty of steamy sex scenes, the purest love, and of course—a guaranteed happy ever after!

This novel contains characters from another of my books, Evergreen. Check that out for Emory and Dante's love story…

Maia

I never thought I would feel happy again. Not one moment. Not after he took my daughter.
The man I married wasn't who I thought he was and he showed me that in the worst possible way.
I was left with nothing, and for five long years that was the way I wanted it...
But now...
I want my life back, but not here, not in Manhattan.
I need to be country away from this place. I'm starting again in Seattle.
A new state, a new home, a new career.
I just didn't expect to find new love...
Atom. He's gorgeous, sexy and mouthwatering and he makes me wat to be very, very naughty...
Do I want to risk my peace of mind for some incredible, mind blowing sex?
Yes.
But can I ever trust another man again?
Atom Harcourt makes me want to try...

Atom

I never believed in love at first sight, not until I met

It was just one moment at a Christmas party forever ago, but I haven't been able to stop thinking about her since that night.

So imagine my surprise when Maia Gahanna turns up in my old hometown, single and looking more beautiful than I remembered—as if that was possible.

But it isn't just that exquisite face… it's her humor, her sweetness, her downright bravery in the face of the worst kind of betrayal.

She is who I've been waiting for, she is the one…

But someone is trying to take my love away from me and that, brother, ain't gonna happen.

I'll fight for her, I'll protect her.

We were meant to be together, that much I know for sure and I'll do anything to make her secure, anything to make her safe…

Anything… anything… to make Maia happy.

She is my world and no-one is going to ruin our love story…

… no-one.

Prolog

Two days before Christmas, New York tech billionaire Zach Konta leaves his Upper East Side home in Manhattan and waves goodbye to his beautiful, much younger wife, Maia. A loving father, Zach is smiling and blowing kisses as he and their five-year-old daughter, Luka, leave to go Christmas shopping for Maia's gifts.

They never return home.

Five years later, after learning that the police are no longer investigating the disappearance and are assuming Zach and Luka are dead, Maia realizes she has to move on with her life. But rumor and suspicion dog her every move, her old friends have drifted away, and eventually she leaves New York and her old life behind to start again on a small coastal island in Washington state. Opening a small bookstore in the little town, Maia soon finds herself warming to her new home and to the new friends she meets there and hopes to leave the terrible grief of her past behind.

Enigmatic architect Atom Harcourt has his own demons to battle. Reeling from the sudden death of his father, a man never satisfied with his son's successes, Atom is looking for anonymity and solitude. When a friend commissions him to build a private home on the island, he hopes to blend in, but he quickly attracts the attention of the island's female population.

But Atom isn't looking for romance. Instead, pursuing commitment-free hookups, he goes to anonymous sex clubs and sleeps with beautiful women whose names he doesn't bother to learn. But then he meets the most beautiful woman he has ever seen, and his heart begins to yearn for something he has never had—a soulmate.

Soon Atom and Maia are falling hard for each other, and both have to decide whether they can trust enough to make a relationship work. After a few missteps, they begin to build a life together but then a series of weird occurrences begin to destroy Maia's peace of mind.

Maia's world is turned upside down as she begins to think that her daughter might be alive—as well as her ex-husband—and it soon becomes clear that someone is trying to hurt her and destroy her new life. Maia and Atom fight to find out the truth before the killer finally comes for Maia, and Atom loses the love of his life… forever.

Chapter One

Maia rolled over onto her stomach and pretended she didn't see her five-year-old daughter creeping into her parents' bedroom. Luka, her long dark hair, so like her mother's, messy and tangled, clouded around her sweet, chubby face as she tried not to giggle.
Maia waited until Luka climbed up onto the end of the bed and was creeping towards the pillows before she reared up, roaring, making her daughter scream and laugh as Maia tickled her.
Maia finally relented and scooped Luka up into her arms, blowing raspberries on her cheeks then nuzzling her nose against her daughter's. "Good morning, Nugget."
Luka giggled, wriggling so she could lock her arms around Maia's neck. "How many sleeps now, Momma?"
Maia grinned. "Seven, sweetie." It was a week before Christmas, and Luka had been nagging at her parents to get a tree and decorate it. "Almost everyone else has already had theirs up for weeks, Momma."

"I know, sweetie, but you know what Daddy's like. He says it spoils it if we celebrate too soon."

But today, a week before Christmas, she and Luka had the whole day planned out. The tree was being delivered to their Upper East Side apartment later that morning, and they had already shopped for way too many ornaments and fairy lights. Luka was almost beside herself with excitement.

Maia got herself and Luka showered and dressed for the day before heading to their kitchen. Their cook, Joelle, smiled at them. "Today's the day, huh?"

While Luka ate her breakfast, Maia checked her messages. Zachary, a proven workaholic, was already at work, but he'd found the time to send her a message despite being the CEO of a multi-national tech company.

Hi darling, have a wonderful day with Nugget today. I love you. Z

Maia smiled to herself. Many people had told her they thought maybe Zach was too aloof for her fun-loving nature, or he seemed distant when they were at parties, but Maia knew that her husband of six years was merely shy. When they were alone, they sincerely enjoyed each other's company, and Maia thought he reined in some of her wilder tendencies.

Maia Gahanna met Zachary Konta when the elusive tech billionaire arrived at her prestigious Manhattan publishing house to discuss his biography.

Maia, then a subeditor of non-fiction, had attended that meeting, shadowing her boss and mentor, Eliza Pentland. She hadn't expected to contribute much, but the moment

Zach Konta had stepped into the room, his eyes had settled on Maia and never left.

Maia had been uncomfortable with his scrutiny, especially when her boss Eliza seemed pissed at her. She deliberately didn't speak to Konta, but an hour after he left her boardroom, a vast bouquet of flowers arrived for her with a note.

Dinner? I'm not the kind of man who takes no for an answer.

Maia had raised an eyebrow at that. Well, there's always a first time for everything, Mr. Konta. She had been all set to call him and refuse his invitation, but Eliza had spotted the bouquet and read the note before Maia could stop her.

Maia told her boss she was refusing the date, and to her surprise, Eliza shook her head. "No, keep it. Maia, we need this book deal with him."

Maia had been shocked, and Eliza held up her hands. "I don't mean sleep with him! Of course not, but a working dinner… he was obviously taken with you, and as a client, he could be valuable to this company."

There was an implied threat in her words—come through for me or your job could be at risk—and so, reluctantly, Maia agreed to have dinner with Konta.

Maia smiled to herself now. She hadn't stood a chance. Zachary Konta was handsome, charming, and attentive. That first dinner turned into a second and a third, and within three months they were married. Now, seven years on, Maia still felt the whiplash from Zach's full-on love bombing.

Maia had grown up in a children's home on Long Island and had been through a number of foster homes before finally striking out on her own. By working three jobs and getting bogged down with student loans, she'd put herself through college, even gaining a scholarship to Columbia, and by hustling and interning, had landed herself a junior editorship at Pentland and Cops Publishing House.

Eliza had been a thorough but fair mentor, but she and Maia were never close. Her aloof exterior did warm, though, after Maia's marriage. Eliza recognized the potential of being in Zachary Konta's social circle. Always good-natured and generous, Maia accepted her new position in society with ease and grace and didn't care that Eliza was using her to improve her own situation. It didn't have any effect on the happiness Maia felt with Zach.

He was twenty years her senior, forty-eight to her twenty-eight, and they celebrated their seventh wedding anniversary a month ago. Their greatest joy in life, though, was undoubtedly Luka. Their precocious, loving daughter had brought them closer together.

The only dark cloud on their seemingly perfect lives was Zach's health. A year ago, he'd been diagnosed with a mild depression, and sometimes, the black moods took him to a place that scared his wife. He would become withdrawn, irritable, and a little possessive of Maia. She weathered his moods with love and patience, and eventually he would emerge, apologetic and remorseful. Today, she and Luka would go shopping for gifts for him. When they were first married, she was at a loss to know what to buy the billionaire husband who could afford anything, obviously, but soon she learned all he wanted was her company and that of Luka's.

Zach, liked her, loved to read, and so when Luka was bundled up against the December cold, they went to their favorite bookstore to find something for his gift. Gerry, the bookstore owner, greeted them with a smile. "Maia, you're in luck. I've just come back from antiquing in Connecticut, and you'll never guess what I found."

He rummaged around the cash register and pulled out a book, handing it to her. Maia smoothed the leather cover. Solaris by Stanislaw Lem. One of Zach's favorite authors. She smiled up at Gerry. "Really?"

"First edition, too. I thought of you immediately."

"This is perfect, Gerry. Thank you. Nugget, why don't you try to find something you would like as a treat while I talk to Gerry?"

Luka smiled and wandered over to the children's section. Gerry's bookstore was a small, independent place with oiled wood shelving and books that weren't just from the New York Times Bestseller List. Maia and Luka could spend hours in the store, and Gerry was so laid back, he never minded. With the store so small, he and Maia could chat while keeping an eye on Luka.

Maia paid for the Lem book and Luka's treat, and they waved goodbye to Gerry, wishing him a happy holiday.

They held hands, swinging them gently as they walked to the different stores. After an hour of strolling, Maia took Luka to a coffee shop and bought her some hot chocolate.

Her phone rang as she was served with her tea, and Maia smiled gratefully at the waitress. "Hello?"

"Hello darling, it's me."

Maia smothered a grin. Who else? "Hey honey."

"I just wanted to remind you about the party tonight."

"I remembered, sweetheart. Nugget and I are going to go find me some shoes soon."

Zach chuckled. "Any excuse."

Maia frowned a little. What was that supposed to mean? She was hardly a spendthrift. "Well, you know I always want to look my best for you."

"I meant nothing by that, sweetie. Sorry, I was distracted for a moment. And you could turn up in a garbage bag and still be the most beautiful woman in the room."

"Ha," Maia flushed at the compliment, her anger forgotten, "Have you been drinking? This early, Mr. Konta?"

Zach laughed. "It's true, regardless. Anyway, I was just checking in. That's my excuse to talk to you. Is Nugget enjoying shopping?"

Maia handed the phone to her daughter. "Dadda wants to say hello."

She listened, smiling, to the conversation Luka had with her father. She was still smiling when Luka handed the phone back.

"See? How we're going to get her to sleep for the next week, I don't know. Do people still disapprove of drugging your kids?" She crossed her eyes at Luka to show she was kidding, making her daughter giggle.
Zach laughed. "I think it might be frowned upon. Look, baby, I have to go. I'll see you later, okay? I love you."
"Love you, too."

They shopped for another hour or so, then went home. Maia had taken some time off from the office for the holidays, having been a workaholic throughout her pregnancy and Luka's formative years. She regretted that now, but at the time, she had wanted to prove to the world and to herself that she was a modern woman—that she could do it. Mostly, she had to admit, she had wanted to prove to those people in Zach's social circle that she wasn't a gold digger, that she had her own agency, that Zach wasn't her sugar daddy. Ugh, she hated that saying. In the last store, she sought out the assistant's help as she tried on shoes for the party. Maia loathed wearing heels, but knew flats were a no-no, so she enlisted help to find some heels that were semi-comfortable at least. Luka played with the empty shoe boxes and helped the assistant sort them back into the right ones before getting bored and wandering off to look at the sparkly kids shoes.
Maia, who hated shopping for shoes, was losing the will to live, and the assistant grinned at her. "You hate this."
"Yup."
"I would, too… well, look, what color is your outfit?"

Maia smiled. "Midnight blue."
They went through a few options while Maia had one eye on Luka. The assistant brought out a final option, and Maia's eyebrows shot up. "Wow, really?"
The assistant held out a pair of what Maia could only describe as Dorothy's ruby slippers. She grinned at Maia. "It's Christmas. Plus, who doesn't need some glitter in their lives?"
The shoes were gorgeous, but not quite fitting for the Upper East Side—but what the hell, Maia thought with a chuckle. "I'll take them."
She glanced over at the children's section—and her heart failed. Her daughter was nowhere to be seen.
Luka was gone.

Chapter Two

"Luka?" She darted over and looked around, panic building. "Luka, honey?" Her voice was rising. "Sweetheart, don't hide now…"
The assistant came over, a concerned look on her face. "Is everything okay?"
Terrified now, Maia looked at her, her eyes wild. "My daughter…"
"Momma!"
Maia whirled around to see Luka jump out from behind a pillar, Zach grinning behind her. Maia's heart began to slow, but now she was annoyed. "Don't ever do that," she said, glaring more at her husband than her daughter. She saw Luka's face drop and hurriedly bent down to her height. "Sweetheart, it's just I was worried."
"Daddy said it would be fun." Luka looked between her mother and father uncertainly.
"Don't worry, sweetie, Momma's just being silly. It was a prank, Maia, that's all."

Maia glared at Zach, her anger simmering. What the hell was wrong with him? Did he think he was funny? And what the hell was he doing here?

Biting her tongue, she returned to the cashier and paid for her shoes, and the family left to go home. Luka was subdued now, and Maia knew she had picked up on the tension between her parents.

To distract her daughter, Maia suggested they go to Rockefeller Center and see the tree there, and that seemed to work. Maia picked up her daughter and hugged her tightly, trying to hide how annoyed she was with Zach. She didn't speak to him directly the entire time.

At home, Luka went to play in her room, and Maia and Zach went to change for the party that evening.

After a few moments of tense silence, Zach sighed. "Maia… come on. It was just a dumb prank."

"Making me think I'd lost my daughter, Zach? That's not a prank, it's just… cruel. Why on earth…" Maia's voice was rising. Was she being too hard on him? Had it really just been a thoughtless joke? "Don't ever do it again."

"Believe me, I won't." Zach muttered, stalking into the bathroom.

Great, Maia thought, still annoyed. Now we'll have an entire evening of snarking and tension. She was still pissed—did Zach think an apology was beneath him? She changed into her dress and did her makeup while Zach was in the shower, then went to find Luka. The little girl was laying in her book nook, reading one of her

favorite stories. Not caring about her dress, Maia crawled inside with her and kissed her. "You okay, Nugget?" Luka nodded, but Maia could see the wariness in her eyes. "Look, darling, it's okay. Daddy just didn't know I'd be so upset, but you know, it's only because the thought of losing you, of never seeing you again, would break my heart, you know? I love you so, so much, Nugget, more than anything in this world. Don't be sad. Sometimes people do things that they think might be funny, but really, they're not. Daddy made a mistake is all. It's okay."
"Momma… are you and Daddy going to split up?"
"No! Gosh, Luka, no… sometimes people have arguments, but they don't last. I love Daddy and he loves both of us. No biggie, okay?"
"No biggie?"
"No biggie." Maia kissed Luka's cute button nose. "Sarah will be here soon, and she called me earlier and told me she's bringing some crafts for you two to do together. So, you can stay up a little later than normal, okay? For a treat."
Luka's eyes lit up. "Okay."

When Maia crawled back out of the book nook, her heart felt eased. Zach was waiting for her, smiling. He helped her to her feet and drew her close. "I'm sorry, Maia. I was an idiot."
He kissed her gently, and she felt the last of her anger slip away. "You're forgiven."
His kiss grew deeper. "I love you, Mrs. Konta."
She chuckled. "Right back at you, Mr. Konta."

They went back to their bedroom to finish dressing and to Maia's surprise, Zach loved her sparkly Dorothy shoes. "That'll show those stuck-up bitches. You look beautiful, darling."
And for once, she felt beautiful. Maia checked her reflection one last time. Her caramel skin, inherited from her Indian mother and Creole father, glowed with the light makeup she had put on, and her long dark hair fell in soft waves down her back. The midnight-blue dress clung to her full breasts, flat stomach, and curvy hips. She wasn't the tallest woman—only five-foot-four—but the heels gave her an extra inch or so next to Zach's six feet. He was gloriously elegant in a dark blue suit, and he took her hand as they said goodbye to Luka and Sarah the sitter and went down to the waiting limousine.

Maia unconsciously straightened her spine as they walked into the party. Even though she knew these people well, she still felt like an outsider. She hadn't been born into this world; she had married into it, and she suspected many of Zach's contemporaries looked down at her. There was one woman, in particular, who repeatedly made it clear that Maia didn't belong and never had. Tracey Golding-Hamm, a stick-thin blonde socialite, beautiful in a pinched, snooty way, had always harbored a crush on Zach and when he'd married the decidedly non-snooty Maia, Tracey hadn't even attempted to hide her disdain. Maia wasn't scared of her; she just hated being in the same room as the vicious blonde.

The couple throwing the party, however, were two people she did like and respect. Henry Klein was Zach's college roommate and business partner, and his wife, Sakata, was a charity maven who actually did more than just throw parties for show. Sakata and Maia had hit it off immediately; as Sakata put it, they were the 'Asian contingent'. Maia had laughed at her description and nodded. "We represent, all right."

Sakata also had no time for the bitchier members of their circle, those men and women who looked down on Maia when she married Zach. "Girl, you have two college degrees, and you're a major force at your publishing company. And you did it on your own. Those jerks have never had to try."

Maia spotted Tracey making a beeline for her and Zach and excused herself. The mood she was in, she didn't want anything to do with the vile bitch.

Coming to her rescue, Sakata bore Maia off as soon as they joined the party. "Come with me; I know where Henry's hidden the good booze."

She and Maia retreated to the kitchen and found a bottle of scotch. Sakata waved it triumphantly. "Henry will kill me but who cares? I have to put up with his crappy taste in wine."

Sakata and Henry enjoyed a rambunctious relationship, forever play-fighting and fooling around. Henry was so easy going and Sakata so mischievous that they seemed incongruous in this world, but Maia wished her own husband was a little more like Henry, fun-loving and chilled out.

But then again... she told Sakata about Zach's prank. "Am I overreacting?"

Sakata pulled a face. "No way. What a jerk move."

Maia felt a little better. "Right? I wanted to kill him."

"I would have certainly made sure I kneed him somewhere painful."

Maia snorted with laughter. "Damn, never thought of that."

Sakata speared an olive from a platter waiting to be taken into the party and popped it in her mouth. "Not like Zachary to play pranks."

"I know. Maybe that's why it shocked me." Maia took a slug of scotch and grimaced. "Ugh."

Sakata snorted. "Yup. Best to sip that one. How did Zach know you were in that store?"

"He said he was just passing and saw us."

"Random."

Maia nodded. She wasn't sure if she believed Zach's story either, but she had no reason to believe otherwise. He was hardly the type of person to keep tabs on her, but a small chill went up her spine anyway. *Don't be stupid... this is Zach we're talking about—the man you love, the father of your child. You know him better than you know yourself.*

She decided to change the subject. "So, who's coming tonight? Apart from the Witch Queen of Angmar. I've already seen her."

"The usual, both good and bad." Sakata grinned. "Oh, and a few new people. A couple we met when we were in Jakarta for the conference, Julia and Gordon VanDusen.

She's lovely, but he's… well, sweet but grabby so keep your eyes open and duck away when you can. And someone Henry's trying to schmooze, Atom Harcourt."
"Name rings a bell."
"You've probably heard of his father, Alan Harcourt, the property magnate. Atom works for him." Sakata lowered her voice. "He's gorgeous, absolutely to die for, but very closed off and reserved. He brought a date but seems to be content to ignore her and drink on his own. I don't think Henry's going to get very far with him."
Maia already felt a kinship with the newcomer. "I wish I had the balls to go hide out. No offense, but you know how much I hate parties."
"No offense taken. For my work, it's a necessary evil." Sakata studied her. "Talking of work… I hear Eliza might be moving on."
Maia flushed. No one was supposed to know about her impending promotion to editor-in-chief—not even Zach knew. But Sakata had spies in many camps. "Nothing is set in stone yet, so I'm not getting excited about it. I don't want to jinx it."
Sakata squeezed her arm. "It's very well deserved, honey, but my lips are sealed, I promise." She sighed. "Well, let's go and rejoin the party. I'll point out the hunk if he comes out of hiding."
Maia was still giggling when they went back to find their husbands. Zach snaked an arm around Maia's waist. "You look happy."
"Always with you," she said and kissed his cheek. He leaned his forehead against hers.

"Does this mean I'm forgiven?"
Maia smiled. "You're forgiven… and when we get home tonight, I'll show you just how forgiven you are."
His eyebrows shot up and desire glowed in his eyes. "I'll make you keep that promise, Maia Konta."

To Maia's relief, the party was a laid-back affair, and the more aloof people kept to themselves. Sakata introduced Maia to Julia and Gordon, and Maia was delighted to see a mischievous glint in Julia's eyes. Gordon was a little boorish but friendly nonetheless, and Maia warmed to the new couple, inviting them for drinks after the holidays.
"I would love that," Julia confided, leaning in conspiratorially. "Some of these women look—"
"—terrifying?" Maia grinned at her new friend and Julia laughed.
"Yup."
Maia chatted easily with Julia while Zach and Gordon talked business and before they knew it, people were starting to leave. "Is it that late already?"
Maia looked around for Zach who had excused himself while she was occupied. "Excuse me, Julia."
"Good to meet you! Call me after Christmas, promise?"
Maia kissed her cheek. "I promise." She liked the other woman immensely. They chatted for a while, then Henry came to claim his wife to introduce her to some other people.
Maia turned and almost groaned out loud. Tracey was right next to her. "Hello, Maia." She looked her up and down, smirking when she saw her red glittery shoes. "Are

we going for Las Vegas Hooker-style? I had no idea this party was fancy dress."

"Sure you did or you wouldn't have come as a raging bitch." Maia shot back. "You might want to mix up your costumes. That one's getting pretty old." She downed the last of her champagne, gave Tracey her most insincere smile and walked away. Yes. Got her. It was petty, but Goddamn, it was satisfying.

She wandered through the remaining people, trying to find her husband. When she couldn't find him, she went out to the balcony for some air. It was bitterly cold, and she shivered but the fresh, sharp air cleared her head.

"Are you looking for someone?"

Maia whirled around at the sound of his voice. Behind her, a man stood up from one of the balcony chairs. He was tall, easily six-five, and broad-shouldered. His dark brown hair was all loose curls, his eyes a vivid green. Three days of dark scruff defined his utterly perfect face. Maia was aware she was staring but she couldn't help herself. He was the most beautiful man she had ever seen. He half-smiled at her scrutiny. "Believe me, this—" he pointed at his face, "—is a curse, not a blessing."

His eyes were steady on hers, and he reached out and touched her cheek. "An exquisite woman like you must be taken."

Maia swallowed hard and nodded. "I'm looking for my husband."

The man smiled. "Husband. Just my luck."

"Maia?"

She heard Zach's voice behind her and rearranged her expression into a smile. "Hey, darling, I was looking for you. This is—" She turned but the beautiful man had disappeared. "A wonderful view." She finished awkwardly, nodding to the view over Central Park. "Nothing compared to what I'm looking at. Let's go home, darling."

Chapter Three

Zach was so loving and attentive on the way home that Maia forgot about the beautiful man, and by the time they had said goodbye to the sitter and checked on a sleeping Luka, she was tired.
But Zach was already hard for her and he peeled her dress from the shoulders. "Keep the shoes on," he murmured, his lips against her throat.
Maia chuckled, then gasped as he ripped her panties from her and deftly unhooked her bra.
"Christ, you're so gorgeous, my love…" He laid her back on the bed and pushed her legs apart. He unzipped his pants and drew out his already hard cock.
"Do you want me to suck you, baby?" The fact that he was still in his suit while she was naked and exposed was turning Maia on, but Zach shook his head, instead pulling her legs around his waist and thrusting into her. She gasped at the quick violence of it, but soon they found

their rhythm and made love, Maia pulling at Zach's clothes, her lips hungry on his.

She woke in the middle of the night to find the bed empty beside her. She sighed. This had happened a few times over the last few months—Zach was finding it difficult to sleep. She slipped from the bed and padded silently through the apartment to find him. He was sitting in his study, his headphones on, staring out of the window.
Maia slipped her arms around his shoulders and hugged him. He lifted his headphones off, setting them on the desk, taking her hand and drawing her onto his lap. She stroked his face, noting the dark circles under his eyes. "What is it, my love?"
Zach shook his head, holding her close, and she stroked his hair. "Is it me? Am I upsetting you in some way?"
"No, darling. You and Luka are the best things in my world. I'm just feeling…" He gave a choked laugh. "I can't even put it into words. Unsettled. Frustrated."
"With what?"
He shrugged. "Life. I don't think depression has a reason, Maia—it just comes. My mother used to suffer from it, too."
Maia held him close. "You've never told me much about your parents."
"I suppose I haven't."
Maia waited, but he didn't go on. She pressed her lips to his. "Come back to bed, darling. I can help relax you."

His hand slid up her thigh underneath her nightgown. "Why not right here?" He said, his voice ragged with arousal. Maia grinned and straddled him as he pushed her nightgown up over her hips.

Maia freed his cock from his sweatpants, and he guided himself into her, pulling down the strap of her gown and exposing her breast as they made love. He took her nipple into his mouth, sucking on it hard and making her gasp and shiver with pleasure. She rode him hard, moaning his name over and over until they both came. Zach let her lead him back to bed afterward, and she wrapped herself around him, cradling his head against her breasts.

But when she slept, she dreamed of vivid green eyes and a sad smile.

Maia drew her daughter's coat around her. "Keep this buttoned up, Nugget, because it's really cold out there."

Luka nodded, smiling. "It's snowing."

"It is. A white Christmas, how about that?" Maia pulled Luka's favorite hat onto her silky, dark hair. "Now, are you both sure you don't need me to come with you?"

Zach grinned and Luka protested. "No, Momma. How are we supposed to buy you surprises when you're there?"

"I'm just kidding, Nugget." She kissed Luka's plump little cheek. "Be good for your Daddy."

Zach swung Luka up into his arms and kissed Maia. "We'll be fine."

"See you later." She followed them to the door and smiled at them. "Have fun."

Zach stepped into the elevator but then stopped. "Have a happy day, Maia."

She grinned. "Without you two? I'll try but I can't promise anything."

She waved to them as the doors closed, then went back into the apartment. She had some work to catch up on, but really, she wanted to wrap all of Luka's gifts before they got back. Even when they thought Luka was asleep, they did not dare risk wrapping her gifts in the evening time—Maia swore blind that Luka could sniff out a gift from a mile away,

Outside the snow was falling thick with the Manhattan skyline wreathed in clouds, and the light was dim. Maia flicked on the Christmas tree lights and spread paper, tape and bows around her. She turned on Miracle on 34th Street on the huge flat screen television and spent a contented morning wrapping presents, watching the movie, and drinking warm spiced apple juice.

When the gifts were wrapped, she checked the clock. Three p.m. They had given their staff—really only their chef, Patricia, and their cleaner, Hannah—paid vacation time, and although Maia loved the two women, she was happy that she had the apartment to herself. She would make supper for them all: Luka's favorite of meatballs and spaghetti (in truth, it was her own favorite, too) and an apple pie. On Christmas Day, she would cook a turkey, but for now, she set about chopping vegetables and seasoning ground beef and pork for the meatballs.

Finally, she slid the dish into the oven to bake in the tomato sauce and checked the time again, frowning slightly. It was almost six, and she had expected them home before now. She checked her phone—no message. Hesitating slightly, she dialed Zach's number. It went straight to voicemail.

"Hey, honey, if you get this, can you give me a call? Just wondering when I should expect you? Guess you two are having fun, huh? Love you. Give Nugget a kiss from me."

She clicked off and put the phone down on the counter. She expected it to ring straight away, but it stayed silent. Don't panic, everything is fine… it's fine.

She went to draw a bath, thinking it would distract her, but as she lay in the warm water, her phone on the bath next to her, she found she couldn't take her eyes off of it, willing it to ring.

There's nothing to worry about; they're probably just caught up in the fun of it.

But by seven, out of the bath and dressed in her robe, Maia began to feel panic rising. She went through the stores that Zach was likely to go to for her gifts. The bookstore, Chanel, Bergdorf's… hating herself, she went to his desk to see if she could find any clues. Any moment, they'll walk through the door and laugh at me for being so worried… any moment.

She saw an appointment written down on his blotter for one of the more exclusive perfumeries in the city and, taking a deep breath, she called it and explained that her husband had an appointment.

"Yes," the woman on the phone told her, "but I'm afraid Mr. Konta failed to show up for the allotted time." The woman sounded a little pissed, but Maia didn't care. Her heart was cold and frozen. Zach never missed appointments. Without explaining, she hung up on the woman and dialed every one of the stores she would expect Zach to have visited, even the odd random stores they'd only ever been to once.

None of them had seen him. "He would have had our daughter with him," Maia said, desperate now, "A cute kid with a red coat and a blue woolen hat with a pink star on it?"

"I'm sorry, ma'am, but we have thousands and thousands of customers today. It is Christmas Eve."

That was the answer she got from all the stores, and even the smaller stores couldn't help her. She tried Zach's phone again and then called Sakata. She explained why she was calling, trying to keep the panic out of her voice, but Sakata was immediately concerned. "We're coming over. Have you called the police yet?"

"Not yet."

"Do it. We'll be over as soon as we can."

Maia bent double in her chair, trying to pull oxygen into her lungs, trying to quell the panic. This wasn't happening, this wasn't happening. Any moment, Luka would come running into the apartment, calling for her, wrapping her little arms around Maia's neck…

She called the police who were polite but disinterested until she told them who Zach was. Then, miraculously, they got real interested real quick. "We'll send someone over at once, ma'am."

Maia shook her head, smiling grimly. She'd be outraged at their favoritism, but right now, she'd take it. Anything to find Luka. And Zach, of course…

If this was another of his 'pranks'… it was way, way too far. But the cold hand squeezing her heart told her this was no prank, no sick joke.

Sakata and Henry arrived just as two detectives appeared at her door, and Maia went through her worries with them and what she'd done to try to find her husband and daughter. To their credit, they assured her that they would follow every lead.

"Aren't we supposed to wait twenty-four hours?" What was she saying? Maia felt her composure slipping. She wanted to scream at them to go, go find her child and her husband, but that came out instead.

Sakata put her arms around Maia as she started to sob, and Maia heard Henry talk quietly to the two detectives.

"Look, obviously, this is very worrying for Maia."

"It's okay, sir. Ma'am, when a minor child is involved, we don't wait the twenty-four hours."

"Thank you, thank you, please, she's just a little girl." Maia wasn't sure if they could understand her through her sobs, but the detective nodded.

"We'll stay in touch, don't worry."

The night closed in and there was no word. Maia redialed Zach's phone a hundred times, but soon the voicemail was full, and she was talking to dead air.

Eventually Sakata called a doctor and although Maia protested, she eventually let him give her a sedative. It didn't knock her out though, but she lay on her bed, her ears straining for any news, ready to hear Luka's sweet voice calling for her.

But there was nothing. As dawn broke, Sakata brought her hot tea. Maia sipped it gratefully. "You've gone over and above for me," she told her friend. "I can't ask you to stay."
"You can, and anyway, I'm not leaving. Henry's gone out to search everywhere he can think of."
"He has?" Maia felt a rush of gratitude. She held Sakata's hand. "Do you think—"
"No. They're fine. There's a perfectly reasonable explanation for this. You'll see…" Sakata's voice broke a little, and she looked away. It made Maia's heart constrict; Sakata knew, like her, that this wasn't good. This wasn't normal.
It was Christmas Day. Maia got out of bed and went into the living room. Seeing Luka's gifts under the tree made her falter, her whole body shaking. "Oh God…" She sank to her knees. "She's gone, isn't she?"
Sakata came to her, and they wept together, Sakata unable to give her friend false hope, and Maia was strangely grateful for it. She didn't want to hope, didn't want the pain of believing her daughter would be returned to her safe and well, because if it didn't happen…
It was unimaginable, but it was happening right now. Luka and Zach were missing.

Hours stretched into days. New Year's came and went, and the world went on around Maia as if her whole life hadn't been ripped apart. She'd sent Sakata and Henry home at last, grateful for their love and support but told them she couldn't ask any more of them.
She had no one else to turn to. Her colleagues, her friends, all of them offered but Maia wanted to be alone—alone so she could scream, alone so she could go out walking in the middle of the night searching everywhere she could think of for any sign of Luka and Zach without anyone stopping her.
One of the things she and Zach had bonded over was that neither of them had a family. Maia had been given up at birth by her mother and had gone through the foster care system. Zach's parents had died in a car wreck when he was seventeen, leaving him a vast fortune but alone in the world. Any other relatives had drifted away when they discovered he wouldn't share the money with their deadbeat asses. It had been one of their greatest regrets that Luka didn't have grandparents, especially when she started kindergarten and came home in tears, asking them why every other child did.
Maia went into her daughter's room now and lay down, burying her face in the pillow, breathing in the powdery sweet scent of Luka's hair. The pain in Maia's soul was searing, burning hot as hell. She couldn't believe she would never see her precious Luka again, nor her husband…

Three days later, the police came to see her and told her they'd found Zach's car abandoned at the side of a bridge on the Cornell University Campus, his alma mater. Inside the car was Luka's backpack and a note to Maia simply saying, "I'm sorry."

There was no sedative the doctor could give Maia that had any chance of containing her raw, desiccating grief at the finality of it.

Luka and Zach were gone.

Chapter Chapter Four

Five Years Later…
Seattle

Atom Harcourt nodded as the judge granted his divorce. He didn't look at Gail as she stood across the room from him. He already knew what her expression would be. Pain, betrayal, hatred. And he deserved it all. Gail was a good woman, and he'd been selfish enough to marry her just to make his father happy. It hadn't worked.
Now his father was gone, and Gail loathed the very sight of him. I'm sorry, he wanted to tell her, I'm sorry I'm such a weak bastard.
He risked a look at her. Her elegant, patrician features were blank as she stared back at him, but her eyes told him the story of her sadness and pain.
God, I'm sorry…
He stepped towards her as the judge dismissed the court, but Gail turned her head and stalked out, ignoring him.

He knew she would never talk to him again, and he didn't blame her.

Atom thanked his lawyer and left quickly, slipping into his Mercedes and driving out of the city. He kept driving in no particular direction until he reached the coastline, then, ignoring the fact he was wearing a seventeen-thousand-dollar handmade suit, he walked along the beach for miles. Even when it started to rain he didn't turn back, grateful that the bad weather meant he was alone.

And he was alone. In the week since his father had died, Atom had been in denial, but now he knew it was the case. His mother had died when he was a kid, and his older brother disappeared into the Australian interior years before and didn't keep in touch. For years it had been Atom and his father, locked in some kind of twisted power play between father and son, always trying to one-up each other.

And Atom was tired of it. His father's death had released something inside of him, a freedom… a kind of relief. The guilt that brought was almost unbearable.

What a fucked-up life. Atom slowed down, breathing hard. He might be wealthy beyond reason, handsome as Adonis, but that was nothing to Atom. He wanted…

What did he want? Marriage clearly wasn't for him. He spent his twenties and thirties fucking his way around the world's most beautiful women, but that hadn't made him happy. He'd been seeking someone who didn't exist. A soulmate.

Only once had he felt the promise of something more—a brief moment at a party five years ago. A moment on a cold December night at an acquaintance's' party.

Her eyes, those large deep brown eyes, wreathed with dark lashes. Her sweet smile. God, it had been less than a minute, but she'd haunted his dreams ever since.

Stupidly. She was married for Chrissakes. After the party, Atom had flown back to Seattle and tried to forget her, but now and again her face would fill his dreams.

Lately, in an effort to assuage his loneliness, he'd begun to frequent sex clubs, the more exclusive ones deep in the city. Anonymous and discreet, he indulged in as much sex as he wanted, without ever having to know the name of the woman he was fucking.

He preferred it that way.

Atom rubbed his face now. Christ, he was so messed up. Something had to change in his life. Something had to give him purpose.

He drove back to his apartment in the city. In the shower, he held his face up to the cool spray, hoping to clear his head. He was meeting an old friend this evening, Dante Harper, who'd just moved back to the city with his wife Emory. The couple had spent a few years in Dante's mother's home country of Italy but were now back in Seattle. Atom and Dante had been close friends as children, and now Atom felt a wave of hope. Dante had always been a steadying force in his life—maybe he could confide in his friend and seek guidance.

Something had to change, that much Atom knew. He just didn't know what to do to change it.

"Atom!" Dante hugged his old friend tightly, and Atom felt his heart lift. Dante introduced him to the lovely woman at his side. "Atom, this is my Emory."
Atom kissed her cheek. "So, it's you who's made this old man so happy? Good to meet you at last."
Emory Harper smiled at him. "And you, Atom. Dante talks about you all the time."
She was beautiful, and Atom felt a pang. Her caramel skin, her large dark eyes… she reminded him of the girl on the balcony.
Over dinner, he learned that the couple had a daughter. "She's eight now and a handful," Emory laughed, showing him a picture of a young girl with merry, dancing eyes and a bright smile "Nella. She keeps asking us for a brother or sister."
"Will you give her one?"
"Nella was adopted," Emory said, matter-of-factly, "I couldn't have children naturally. But we're thinking about adopting again." She grinned at Dante. "Just depends on whether my old man has the energy."
Dante laughed. "Enough with the 'old man'." He looked at Atom. "And what about you?"
Atom shrugged and told them about the divorce. "It was for the best."
"So recent though." Emory frowned at him. "Are you okay?"

No. No, I'm not okay. Not by a long shot. "I'm fine. Start of a new era." He looked at Dante. "Maybe you can suggest a new project for us to do together? I need a new challenge."

Dante and Emory exchanged a glance, and Dante nodded. "I'm sure we can come up with something."

"Atom… when we're settled in the new house, you'll have to come and stay with us for a weekend. If we ever find somewhere. We're looking at places out on Bainbridge Island."

"I can help with that," he told them. "I have contacts in the area."

After he'd said goodbye to his friends, he intended to drive home but instead drove into the city to one of his favorite clubs—a club that asked their clients to wear masquerade eye masks for the ultimate anonymity. He sat at the bar for a while before being welcomed into the rooms at the back of the club. It was another bar, but this time, the clientele wasn't there for cocktails.

As Atom fixed the masquerade mask over his eyes, he passed his gaze over the women there. He had already slept with a few of them, and some of them, he knew, wouldn't mind revisiting their trysts, but he never slept with the same woman twice—he'd made that known right at the beginning.

His eyes were drawn to a dark-haired woman seated at the bar. She was new. Her curves were poured into a skin-tight red dress which clung to her small waist and rounded hips. Her breasts were full and beautifully shaped. Atom felt his cock respond to her beauty. Her face was almost completely obscured by her white mask, but he could see her full, rose-pink mouth as she sipped her drink.

He went over, ordered a mineral water and sat down next to her. She didn't look at him, and when she picked her glass up, he could see her hands trembling. Ah. So, she was really new… and inexperienced at this.

"Hello."

She turned unnaturally violet eyes to him—contacts, he guessed. She really didn't want anyone to see the real her and that intrigued him. "Hello." A soft voice, a slight quaver.

He smiled, his eyes soft. "You're new here."

She nodded. "I am. I…" She gave a sweet little chuckle. "I don't really know what I'm doing here. It was a whim. I'm sorry, I should probably be all cool and confident, but the truth is… I have no idea what I'm doing." She shook her head, smiling. "I think I'm out of my depth here. I was just trying something different, you know? Something out of my comfort zone."

Atom touched a finger to her cheek, was gratified when she didn't pull away. There was something compelling about this woman, about her honesty. Usually, the people at the club put on an act—which was kind of the point of the masks—but this woman…

"If you're not comfortable, lovely lady…"

"I should go."

Atom felt bereft, but he nodded. "I would hate it if you were caught up in something you weren't ready for."

What was he saying? When had he turned into a bleeding heart? But something about her made him feel protective. She was gorgeous, sexy… and definitely in the wrong place. "May I walk you out?"

She hesitated, then nodded, and he offered her his arm. "I have to say, I'm surprised to find such a gentleman here. Thank you."

"You're welcome." Ask her for her number. Ask her to come home with you. Don't let her go. "Can I drive you home?"

Uh oh, wrong thing to say. He saw wariness in her eyes, and he held up his hands. "Forget I said that, I'm sorry. I meant it well, not as the awkward come-on it sounded like."

She gave a small laugh of relief. "It's okay, I'll take a cab." Atom waited outside the club with her until they hailed a cab, then opened the door for her. "It was good to meet you."

"And you. Thank you rescuing me from that place." She hesitated then quickly kissed him, brief, soft on the mouth. "For what it's worth, you made this evening a good one. Goodbye."

"Bye."

He watched as the cab drove away and shook his head. What a freaking weird night. When the cab had disappeared into the night, Atom took off his mask, showing it into his pocket. He'd lost the enthusiasm for casual sex tonight. He went to his car, thankful he hadn't had anything alcoholic to drink. He wanted to drive in the cool air of the night to clear his head. His lips still tingled from the soft kiss, her soft kiss...

"Ah, damn it." What was wrong with him? Twice now, he'd been in the company of a woman who had aroused in him not just sexual feelings, but something else, something deeper, and both times he'd let her go.

Fuck.

Maybe it was time to grow up and try to find someone who meant something more than a quick hook-up, someone he could really care about.

Maybe it was time.

Chapter Five

Maia thanked the cab driver and let herself into her hotel room. She stripped out of the red dress, and with relief, removed the violet contacts from her eyes. She was still trembling and when she'd showered and changed into sweats, she crawled onto the bed and let out a sigh.
"What the hell was I thinking?" Earlier, feeling brave—and frustrated—going to the club had seemed like a good idea. She had needed to feel the touch of another human, had needed it for a couple of years now, and tonight, her frustration had peaked, and she'd done her research on the internet.
Anonymous, masked sex sounded kinky and a good option. Maybe if the guy in the club hadn't been so kind, she would have gone through with it. She smiled to herself then. Yeah, he'd been a sweetie, and thank God for it.

Maia sat back against the headboard. At least she'd been saved from a train wreck. Her biggest train wreck of course was her life now. After five years of nothing but searching for Luka and Zach, not believing her daughter was gone, her friends had sat her down.

Sakata, Julia… they'd both told her some harsh truths. "They're gone," Sakata had said, holding Maia's hands. "Luka is gone. Dead, Maia. Zach's note made that clear." Maia winced now recalling it, but she had known they were right. "You need to make a new life now, my darling," Julia, who'd become a good friend, told her. "Away from New York."

She had known they were right about that, too. Her nemesis Tracey had been crowing to anyone who would listen about how Maia couldn't keep her husband happy, that she'd made him so desperate he killed himself and his daughter. There was more than one occasion when Maia had been held back from going full medieval on Tracey's smug ass. The final straw was the article in one of New York's high-end magazines. The article was clearly planted by Tracey and painted Maia as nothing more than a gold-digging whore. Maia's friend leapt to her defense and encouraged her to sue the writer and the magazine, but Maia was exhausted by all of it.

So, she'd chosen to move across the country. She'd never been to Seattle before, but as soon as she saw the waters of Elliott Bay and Puget Sound, the Olympic mountains, and Mount Rainier so majestic against the skyline, she knew she had made the right decision.

A new life.

The New York police were still refusing to close the case and declare Zach and Luka dead.

Zach… she would never forgive him. Ever. It was as simple as that. When, at his memorial, his friends had extolled on what a great man he was, she could hardly stop herself from screaming out that he was a murderer. That he had taken her daughter away—ended her young life for no other reason than to cause Maia pain.

Bastard.

So, Maia, her anger, her hurt a burning thing, divorced Zach in absentia, and in her divorce filing asked for sole custody of Luka… the daughter who was lost. Zach's money was tied up, but she'd had enough saved of her own—and the apartment had been in her name for tax reasons—that she sold everything, readying for the move out to the West Coast.

She'd given Henry full control of Zach's part in the company, not caring to run it herself, but wanting to save some of Luka's inheritance… just in case.

Everything was 'just in case,' but with every day that passed, Maia began to accept she would never see her daughter again.

Now, she had been in Seattle for a few days, and for the time being, she had holed up in a small but clean hotel. She had some vague idea about what she wanted to do, but she'd lost confidence in herself. After the disappearance, she had given up her position at the publishing company, spending every day searching for any clue to Luka's fate.

She'd driven herself half mad.

Now, as she began to accept that Luka was gone, and as she stood on the edge of a new life, there was a small glimmer of optimism in her soul. There were good people in this world; the stranger at the sex club had proved that.

Two days later, she was standing in an empty storefront on Bainbridge Island. From the large picture windows, she could see across the bay to the city. The polished wooden floors and shelves smelled wonderful, and Maia knew she had found her place. She talked about the lease with the realtor and ended up signing a five-year contract.

"What will you do with the place?" The realtor, Jensen, was looking at her with interest, a cute young man with dark blonde hair and merry green eyes.

"A bookshop," she said, smiling at him. "I know that must sound boring to you, but I love reading."

"Not at all," he assured her. "I'm a nerd, too. Oh, I mean… no offense." He seemed to realize she might take that as an insult, but Maia laughed.

"None taken, I am a nerd and proud of it." She looked around her new premises. "Now, business done. Let's talk about somewhere to live."

Jensen came through for her again with a home: he found her a small house on a quiet street with a garden that led down to a tiny private beach. It had been up for rent for a while, the furniture covered in dust sheets, but as Maia walked through it, she could see herself here.

The porch had an old swing, rife with woodworm, but as she sat down gingerly, it swung gently. Jensen was watching her. "Well?"

She smiled at him. "Yes. You had a good day, Jensen."

He laughed. "Glad to hear it. Now, let's get the business out of the way. I know some movers if you need them."

"I don't. I didn't bring anything but my clothes and books with me." Maia stood up. "I'm starting over, Jensen. But if you could point me in the way of a good furniture store, I'd be grateful."

A week later and she had moved in. She found she enjoyed living so sparsely, so when Jensen had hooked her up with a great furniture store, she bought a few pieces—a new bed, kitchen table, some comfortable armchairs—but she found herself each evening sitting outside on the rickety porch swing and watching the sunsets over the island.

During the days she scrubbed, polished, and oiled the wooden floors and shelves of her new bookstore, and then enthusiastically filled the shelves. She sought out a sign maker and three weeks after her arrival in Washington, Luka's Books, opened to a curious crowd of buyers.

Atom hugged Emory as she opened the door to him. "Hey, you. You look… better." She studied him and nodded approvingly. Atom grinned at her. Even though they hadn't known each other for a long time, he'd grown very fond of his friend's wife.

Emory Harper had been through the mill when it came to life. Injured in a school massacre, she'd been shot by a vengeful ex-husband and only survived due to Dante's help and care. A former school teacher, she now taught as a professor at UW.

Nella, the Harpers' daughter, greeted Atom shyly. "I think she has a crush on you," Emory grinned to her daughter's protest.

Dante clapped Atom's shoulder. "Just in time. I've been cooking."

"Baby. You put steaks on a grill." Emory chuckled at his pout. "Okay, okay, that counts."

In the garden of their rented home on Bainbridge Island, Atom saw they had indeed started a cookout. Some mutual friends had also made their way to the party, and Atom chatted easily with them.

Emory was right. For the past few weeks, a weight had lifted from Atom's shoulders. No more was the fear of disappointing his father in his life… because the fear of disappointing himself had replaced it.

But that was something he could do something about. He'd been talking to Dante, late into the nights sometimes, and Dante had convinced him that change was already in his own hands.

He'd confided about the girl at the club, and Dante had nodded. "Sometimes people are brought into our lives for a reason. I know Em was, despite the horrific way we met. Em will tell you that everything happens for a reason, and she would know." He patted his friend's shoulder. "This girl, whoever she was, you may never see her again. You probably won't see her again. But just maybe, she taught you that someone could get into that heart of yours."

Atom had thought about his friend's words again and again between then and now, and in his everyday life, he began to see new possibilities, new connections he could make. He wasn't seeking 'the one' relentlessly, just opening his mind to something more than just a fling. Certainly more than what he had given Gail during their marriage. Christ, he'd been a bastard even if he'd never raised his voice or his fist to her. Absence was another kind of abuse. He'd called her and left her a long rambling voicemail message when she didn't pick up, apologizing, but she hadn't called him back. Atom couldn't blame her. She wanted to move past the pain, and he could respect that. It wasn't for Gail to absolve his guilt.

"Hey, buddy." Dante sat down next to him now, beer in hand. "Now that I have a moment off from chef-ing duties—" he grinned as Emory scoffed at him, "I wanted to talk to you about something."

"Go for it."

"We've found some land here on the island, and we'd like you to build us a house."

Atom sipped his beer. "Oh, just that?" He laughed. "Wow, okay…"

"You're the best architect I know, hell, any of us know, and you've spent far too long sitting in meetings and behind desks. Come on, At, you know that's true. With all due respect, your father never gave you the freedom to create like I know you can. So, carte blanche. Unlimited budget. Build my girls a palace."

Atom grinned at his friend. "I'm assuming you're speaking figuratively?"

"You know what I mean. Emory has a ton of ideas, so I'm sure she'll tell you all of them and then some." Dante leaned in and said in a stage-whisper, "I hate to tell you this, but Em has a project book stuffed with ideas. There are turrets, man, turrets!"

"I can hear you." Emory giggled and came to sit on his knee. "So, Atom, Dante's told you?"

"He has, and I'm looking forward to it." Atom smiled at the couple, watching them as they held each other. They were so close, so in sync with each other, and it made Atom's heart ache. Would he ever find someone like that?

As he drove home that night, he wondered if Dante and Emory were so close because they had been through hell together—actual life-and-death crap. He felt bad for feeling so depressed when they had been through much worse than he had ever been through…… that he would admit to, anyway. There were some parts of his life that he had closed off to himself and had denied all his life because they were just too painful to confront.

On the ferry back to the mainland, he looked back over to the island. He liked the pace of life there—it was pretty chill. It was a bedroom community, feeding into the city's businesses, yes, but he liked the feel of the place.

And it was beautiful, too. He was looking forward to building Dante and Emory's new home and while he was out there, maybe he'd rent a place—see how island life suited him.

It was something different. A different way to live his life. His business practically ran itself, thanks to his uber-efficient team, and it wasn't as if he couldn't afford to take time off for a passion project. Thanks to his father's will, he was worth billions.

Atom half-laughed to himself. He had made his own money, albeit with the help of a good education and help from his father, but now, with unlimited resources....

Just don't waste it, he told himself, use it to build a new life, get some passion back. Yes, this new project would change things for him, and it was about time.

With a definite lift in his spirits he went home and straight to bed, dreaming of blueprints, bricks, and a new life.

Chapter Six

No sooner than Maia had put a 'Help Wanted' notice in the bookshop window than a young Asian-American girl came in, smiling shyly. Lark Sun was a college student looking to spend what remained of the summer vacation working and saving for her sophomore year at UW. What began as a formal interview soon turned into talking about their favorite books, and Maia knew she had found the right person. Lark wanted to start as soon as possible, and so Maia and she agreed on her hours and schedule. She thanked Maia for the opportunity, but as she was leaving, Maia called her back. "One more thing… do you like dogs?"
"I love dogs," Lark nodded. "Are you thinking of getting one?"
"I like the idea of a bookshop dog. It adds to the relaxed feel I'm going for. Also, I could use the company at night."

"It's a wonderful idea."

Maia smiled at her new friend. "Good. Then we'll see you on Monday morning."

She closed the store early and drove her rental car to the nearest rescue shelter. Her heart ached for all the poor dogs who needed love and a good, kind home, and she wished she could take them all. But when she saw the spaniel, she knew she was the one. A King Charles Cavalier, ruby and white, gazed up at her with huge brown eyes, and Maia was lost.

Soon, she and the dog were back in the rental car. The spaniel, named Betty, was spread-eagled on the passenger seat, her head laid on Maia's thigh as Maia drove them both back home. Maia brought the dog into the house and let her sniff around where she liked, checking the place out, giving her space.

Maia heated a can of soup for her own supper and gave Betty a dish of dog food, which the dog cleaned out in seconds, making Maia laugh. "Hungry, girl?"

After supper, Maia sat out on the porch with Betty on her lap, stroking the dog's soft ears, and for the first time in what seemed like a lifetime, she felt contentment.

It was late August, and the weather was still warm and sultry, and Maia sat outside for most of the evening, reading her book, and fussing with Betty. The dog wandered in the yard a little, but cleaved close to Maia, the two of them forming a quick bond.

Maia was about to go in after the sun finally set but was stopped by the sound of singing coming from a car that had pulled up across the street. Two teenage girls, all long legs and wide smiles, piled out of a car tunelessly singing a rock song. Betty looked up at the noise, and Maia smiled to herself, the girls' mood infectious.

They noticed her sitting there and waved. She waved back, and they came over. "Hello, you're new."

Maia laughed. "Relatively. Maia Gahanna."

The taller of the two girls grinned. "I'm Michonne, and this is my irritating younger sister, Jamelia. We live over there—" she waved a hand nonchalantly towards the house across the street, "—with our mom. Aw, can I pet your dog? She's gorgeous."

"Of course."

Jamelia smiled shyly at Maia. Both girls were gorgeous with their ebony skin, Michonne with hair pulled back in a ponytail and Jamelia's cropped close to her scalp. They were so tall that Maia felt dwarfed, but both were so outgoing and friendly that she found chatting with them easy.

It was dark before they knew it, and Michonne and Jamelia stood to leave. "Come over and meet Mom soon. She'd love to get to know you. She's Unique."

"Most moms are."

Jamelia grinned. "No, Unique is her name."

"Ah. Well, I look forward to meeting her." Maia picked Betty up. "Goodnight, girls, thanks for making my evening."

They called their goodbyes, grinning and waving, and Maia's heart lifted. Sweet, sweet girls.

She went inside. Betty followed her up the stairs and jumped on the bed, and Maia shrugged. The dog curled up next to her pillow and when Maia returned from brushing her teeth, she laughed at the dog's guilty look. Maia crawled on the bed next to Betty. "You can stay, gorgeous." She stroked Betty's silky head and kissed the tip of her nose. The dog licked her face once, then burrowed into the crook of her neck.

Maia was still smiling as she fell asleep.

Both Lark and Betty proved to be huge successes, and Maia found she loved working in the bookstore, getting to know the locals. Lark had an encyclopedic knowledge of books, especially the young adult section, and she and Maia could spend hours just talking about what they were reading at any given time. Lark also adored Betty, which helped, and Betty enchanted almost everyone who came into the store.

As summer gave way to fall, and the night began to draw in, Maia and Lark decorated the store with Halloween decorations, and Lark began a 'Scary Stories for Children' afternoon.

It was on one of these afternoons that Maia met someone who made her long for her daughter. A beautiful young woman brought her daughter in to the store for the story time, and Maia felt her heart stop. The mother clearly had Indian blood in her, and the little girl she was with— about ten years old, Maia guessed—looked so much like an older Luka that Maia felt her chest clench.

The woman smiled at her, not realizing Maia's distress. "Hi, there. We're not too late, are we?"
Maia swallowed. "Of course not. Lark's just setting up. Hello," she smiled at the young girl. "Would you like a cupcake? These ones are chocolate, the ones with little ghosts on them, and the others are pumpkin spice flavor."
The girl nodded shyly. "Thank you."
Her mother smiled. "This is Nella." She ruffled her daughter's dark hair and held her hand out to Maia. "Emory Harper."
"Maia Gahanna. It's good to meet you both… I'm sorry, I can't remember if I've seen you in here before."
"First time, but we've been meaning to come in for a while. We're new to the island, but not the area. Are you from Seattle?"
Maia shook her head. "New York. I've only been here for a few months, well, two months to be exact, but I have to say, I love it."
Emory beamed at her. "It is wonderful, isn't it? The mountains, the ocean… great place to bring up a child. Nella loves it here."
Maia felt another tug on her heart. "Is she your only child?"
"Yup, so far, but we're thinking of adopting another."
Maia was surprised. "Nella is adopted? She's the image of you."
Emory grinned. "I know. We chose a biracial child deliberately, although until we met Nella, we had no idea

she would look so much like me. Do you have family with you?"

Maia shook her head but said nothing, and Emory didn't press her. They chatted some more, finding common ground, and Maia thought how nice it would be to have Emory as a friend. As if reading her mind, Emory smiled at her. "Would you like to have coffee sometime? I have a feeling you and I could be great friends."

"I would love that," Maia said sincerely, feeling her heart lift. "I really would. Look, here's my cell phone number," she handed a card to Emory. "Let's do it soon."

"You got it."

Emory called her a few days later, and they arranged to meet for coffee at a café on the other side of the island. Emory explained she had found it by accident one day, on a walk from their rented home. "We're actually building a place on the shoreline, but it won't be ready for months. Dream home, so Dante—that's my husband—tells me. I think any home with him and Nella is a dream."

"Do you work?"

"I teach at UW. I used to teach English at Auburn, but now I lecture part-time. Did you have a bookstore in New York?"

Maia told her about her publishing career, and Emory was impressed. "And you didn't want to work in publishing here?"

"I wanted a more laid-back lifestyle." Maia had been practicing that answer, and Emory seemed to buy it.

"Can I ask a question?"

"Of course."

"Have you a partner? I'm being nosy, I know, but you're such a lovely person; it seems strange that you're on your own."

Maia hesitated for a moment. "I was married. He died."

Emory's face went red. "Oh, I'm sorry, I didn't mean to intrude."

Maia held her hands up. "It's okay. It's complicated, really… he took my daughter and disappeared on Christmas Eve five years ago. They found his car with a note next to a bridge."

Emory went pale. "Oh, Maia…"

"Yes. So, the fact is he's dead…" She gave a humorless laugh. "Sorry, you don't want to hear this."

Emory put her hand on Maia's. "Listen, if you need to talk about any of it, please know, I'm here for you. It must be strange coming to a new place and starting over. I admire that."

Maia said goodbye to Emory and drove back to her home. It had felt good to talk about Luka with someone; she had stopped doing that with her friends years ago, the pain too raw. But pretending Luka never existed wasn't an option, and Maia knew that here, she had an opportunity to get the pain out—process it—and start over.

Betty greeted her excitedly as she opened the door, and Maia spent a few minutes fussing over her beloved dog before dropping her keys on the table and heading into

the kitchen. No sooner than she had fed Betty than she heard someone knocking.
Jamelia Benjamin grinned at her. "Hello again, Mom wanted to know if you'd like to come and eat with us. She's made enough for a small army. Bring Betty, too."
Maia was tired, but she couldn't say no to Jamelia's hopeful face and thanked her. "Can I bring anything?"
"Seriously, we have enough food for about a week. Mom's been practicing some new dishes."
On the walk to the Benjamin's house, Jamelia explained that Unique Benjamin was a professional private caterer. "So, it'll all be good, but there'll be a lot of choice."

Jamelia introduced Maia to her mother, a striking African-American woman in her early forties, who appraised Maia and nodded, given her silent approval.
"The girls haven't been bothering you, have they?"
"Not at all, I love their company. Man, that smells good."
Unique smiled. "Well, I'm sure Jam's told you what I do for a living. Come and sit with us."
Over the most delicious supper, Unique and her daughters quizzed Maia on her life. Jamelia soon excused herself from the table to go play with a slavering Betty, who got excited when Jamelia fed her strips of chicken from her plate. Maia grinned, rolling her eyes. "She'll never eat regular doggie chow now."
Unique was studying her. "So, you own a bookstore?"
"I do. Luka's, down by the harbor. Actually, learning that you're a caterer, I have an idea. I've been wanting to add

some refreshments and coffee to the shop—would you be interested?"

Unique smiled. "You're very sweet, but I'm not much of a baker, although I do have a great contact on the island. I promise, you won't be unhappy with her."

"Thank you, that sounds great."

Maia decided that Unique, although friendly, played her cards close to her chest. She wasn't as immediately outgoing as her daughters, but when Maia was leaving, having thanked her host, Unique sent her daughters inside and walked across the street with Maia. "Maia, if you ever feel… alone or afraid in that big house… there'll always be a spare room for you at our place."

Maia was surprised, and Unique laughed at her expression. "I know. I look fiercer than I actually am. As a single mother, I've had to be. I don't make friends easily, but I think you might be the exception. Take care of yourself, Maia."

Emory slipped into bed next to Dante, and he hooked an arm around her shoulders and put down the book he was reading. "Hey, cutie."

She kissed him, sliding her hand down to his groin, feeling his cock responded as she stroked it. "Good evening, sir."

Dante chuckled and rolled her onto her back. Emory cradled his face in her hands. They had been married for ten years now, but every day she fell more in love with him. They shared the same silly sense of humor, the same self-deprecating mischief, and their love for their daughter had brought them even closer.

Dante's mouth closed around her nipple now as she stroked his hair, and he moved down until his face was buried in her sex, and Emory shivered with pleasure as his tongue lashed around her clit, sensation building until she was moaning his name. Dante made her come, then moving up her body, thrust into her. They made love slowly at first, then as their excitement built, they clung to each other and fucked hard, laughing and urging the other on.

Afterward, Dante wrapped his wife in his arms, pressing his lips against her forehead. "Never gonna get tired of doing that with you," he said, and Emory giggled, snuggling in closer to him.

"Ditto, big guy." She stroked his back. "I had coffee with the bookstore owner, Maia, today. She's really great, very sweet."

"Good to know."

Emory chewed on her bottom lip. "I was thinking—"

"—Uh oh."

"Ha-ha, funny boy. Now, really, I was thinking, we should have some friends over for dinner soon. Clem and Maximo, Zea and Flynt. Maia." She left a pause. "Atom."

"Ah." Dante's eyes were twinkling as he grinned at her. "Someone's doing some matchmaking."

"Noooo…" She extended the word way too long but then giggled. "You caught me. I just think… well, it couldn't hurt."

"Hmm. Just promise you won't make it too obvious. I wouldn't want Atom to think we're railroading him. Nor this Maia person."

Emory nodded. "Promise. You know what's weird? She and I could be related. I mean, she's got Indian blood, too, but more than that, we actually look similar." She thought some more about what Maia had told her. "I think she's got a pretty tragic past."

"Another thing you have in common."

Emory smiled. "I got my happy ending."

"And now you want to give this stranger hers?"

"Something like that." Emory laughed and kissed him. "And I have this feeling she won't be a stranger. I really liked her, Dante."

Dante smiled down at her. "I'm glad, sweetheart, but listen, by all means invite her and the others to dinner. Our home is theirs, you know that. Just don't and try force something."

"I swear. Now, put that big fine cock back inside me, Mr. Harper."

Dante grinned, rolling her onto her back and pushing her legs apart with his knee. "Your wish is my command, ma'am."

Atom had gone back to the club, but his only goal was to see if she had come back—if she had found her courage. He hadn't been able to stop thinking about her, and his heart thudded with disappointment when he saw she hadn't returned. He asked the bartender if he'd seen her, but the man had only shaken his head. "No, man. She never came back. Shame, she had a banging body."

Atom had a drink, but then left, to the disappointment of the woman who were circling him, but Atom barely registered them. So, it was twice now in his life that he'd felt that instant connection to someone, to a woman, and he'd blown it the second time, too.

Atom didn't believe in love at first sight but the raw, unnamable bond he had felt to both women… there must be something in it, it must mean something… surely?

"Well… fuck." He said to himself now as he drove home to his silent apartment. He had decided to move out to the island while he oversaw the construction of Dante's home, and most of his stuff had been packed up now. He looked around the bare bones of his home and saw that it reflected how he felt in his heart.

Almost empty.

No, this wasn't going to be his life. The next time he found that connection—and God, how he hoped he would get a third chance—he would act on it. He would make it count.

He would find the one.

Chapter Seven

Maia put Betty into the car and packed the dessert she had bought carefully onto the back seat, praying she wouldn't have to make any unnecessarily sharp stops on the way to Emory's house. It was the week before Halloween, and she was enjoying all the decorated houses and porches as she drove across the island. More and more, this island was becoming a home. Back in Manhattan, in Zach's world, she'd had Sakata and Julia, but she'd always found most of Zach's friends dismissive of her. Here, all of her new friends were so different and yet they shared one vital thing: she believed they cared for her.
And she adored them. Lark, her cohort and buddy at the store, despite the age gap, they were two silly schoolgirls giggling together. Michonne and Jamelia made her feel young, too, always bringing her gifts like a new top they'd found on one of their—many—shopping excursions and

making her watch K-Pop music videos on YouTube with them, sighing over the beautiful boy bands.

Unique had become, if not a mother figure, then certainly a trusted aunt. The older woman was someone Maia could confide in, ask opinions of, ask for advice. Maia would sit with Unique in her kitchen and be her taste tester for the new recipes she was trying out.

But it was Emory whom Maia felt closest to. The two women found common ground in their past histories, even to the point where Emory had told her they had both lost a 'Luka'—in Emory's case it was an old lover, Luca Saffran, who had been murdered by Emory's psychotic ex-husband, a man who had almost killed Emory, too.

Maia was relieved she could talk openly about her daughter—and about her rage for her ex-husband.

"There were no signs," she said to Emory one afternoon when Emory had come to the bookstore. "He was depressed, but why did he have to kill Luka? Why would he do that to me?"

Emory had been sympathetic. "Sometimes we have no idea of the real person we're married to. I suppose, in that way, I was lucky. When Ray turned into the murderous bastard he was, I had the clues, or rather the bruises to foreshadow it."

Emory had told Maia that in the end, she'd had to deal with Ray herself before he killed anyone else, and Maia knew that feeling. "If Zach were still here… I never thought myself capable of killing, but now…"

Emory had hugged her. "Sweetheart, I know."

Maia smiled to herself now as she remembered that hug. Emory was something she'd never had—a sister.

She drew up to the rented house that Emory and Dante had leased, noting the other expensive cars in the driveway. She wondered who she would meet, whether the Harper's clique was as exclusive as Zach's had been. Somehow, she didn't think so.

She took a few deep breaths to quell her nervousness as she rang the bell. Expecting a housekeeper to open the door, she grinned in relief when Emory greeted her with a wide smile. "Maia! Come on in, everyone's here."

Seeing the faint shiver of trepidation in Maia's eyes, Emory smiled. "Don't worry, they're all harmless. It's just the eight of us."

She tucked her arm in Maia's, taking the dessert dish from her. "Peach cobbler? You darling, it's my favorite. Good luck to anyone else getting a taste of this."

They went to the kitchen first, and Maia almost swooned at the layout, huge with picture windows leading onto a garden at one end. Emory grinned. "I know, right? The house we're having built will have an even bigger kitchen, but very much modelled on this one. It was the reason we took this for the time being. Now, come and meet the others."

Atom was talking to Maximo Neri when Emory returned with the newcomer, and if he was aware he was gaping in shock, then he didn't care. The girl from five years ago.

The girl from the balcony. What the hell was she doing in Seattle?

And Christ, she was just as beautiful as she had been back then. Emory was introducing her to Clementine, Maximo's wife. His heart felt like it would beat out of his chest, and he took too big a slug of his champagne and choked. His face burned as everyone turned to look at him. "Sorry." He mumbled it and wiped his chin with his handkerchief as Emory and the beauty approached.

"And here, providing our in-house entertainment," Emory said with a sly grin, "Is Atom. Atom Harcourt, meet Maia Gahanna."

Maia held out her hand, and Atom could see no recognition of him in her eyes. He took her hand, her touch sending waves of pleasure through him. "It's good to meet you. Actually, we have met before."

Something flickered in her eyes then, but she smiled shyly. "We have?"

Ah. That smoky voice, he remembered that… and weirdly, he thought, I've heard it recently. "At Henry and Sakata's party five years ago. On the balcony. You were there with your husband?"

Maia Gahanna was staring at him as if she had seen a ghost. Emory sensed the strange tension and broke it by calling everyone into dinner.

He thought that Emory would seat him beside Maia Gahanna, but then he saw a glance pass between Dante and his wife, and Emory quickly changed her mind, sitting beside Atom herself and sweeping Maia next to Dante.

But Atom had a hard job concentrating on the food as delicious as it was. His eyes were constantly drawn to the beautiful woman across the table. He noticed that whenever she met his gaze, she flushed and looked away, and his body reacted to the blush on her lovely face.

Emory nudged him. "So," she said, trying to hide a grin, "you and Maia have met before?"

"Briefly. She was with her husband." Atom tore his eyes away from Maia for a moment. "He's not around anymore?" He hated that the idea filled him with a strange happiness.

Emory leaned in, lowering her voice. "He died. It's… complicated, but it's not my story to tell. Let's just say, Maia has been through it." She studied him. "You like her."

He nodded. "We had a moment. It remains to be seen whether anything could come of it but thank you for inviting me here tonight."

Emory squeezed his arm. "Tread gently. I know that you will."

Atom didn't get the chance to talk to Maia throughout dinner or afterward as they retired to the living room for brandy, but when Clem and Maximo were leaving, he saw Maia slip back into the house. Waiting a beat, he followed her when she stepped out into the garden of the property.

"It's not quite a balcony, but here we are again." He said it softly, and she turned to look at him. For a moment, she gazed at him then a smile crept over her face.

"We've met since then, Mr. Harcourt."

That stopped him, but suddenly he knew she was right. "Where?"

Maia smiled and his whole body responded. He prayed his erection wouldn't be too obvious. "Somewhere out of my comfort zone."

It took a second, but the realization hit. "The club? That was you?"

She laughed. "It was. And you were the perfect gentleman. Don't worry, I won't say anything to your friends."

Atom stepped closer, gratified when she didn't move away. "I've been thinking about you ever since that night. I even went back to see if you'd been back."

"I haven't. Too chicken—or rather… I don't know. Maybe it's not for me."

"I'm sorry to hear about your husband."

Her smile faded. "Don't be."

Okay, that was weird. "Can I see you again?"

Maia gazed at him. The violet contacts were gone, and her dark chocolatey eyes were warm, soft. "Do you have a pen?"

He reached into his jacket and pulled out a pen, handing it to her. She took hold of his hand and wrote an address on his palm, handing him the pen back afterward. "I'm going home now. I'll wait up until one a.m. If you're not there by then, no harm, no foul."

Atom's eyebrows shot up, but he saw that her cheeks were flushed. She was trying to be brave. "Out of your comfort zone?"

"That remains to be seen." And then, she kissed him, briefly, softly like she had in the club that night, and turned and walked back into the house. Atom heard her saying goodbye to Emory and Dante, then a few moments later, her car start.

Was he going to do this?

He laughed aloud. Hell, yes. Even if nothing actually happened between them—not a likely scenario—but hot damn, he was going to take her up on her invitation. He kissed Emory's cheek and hugged Dante. "Thanks, guys, for a great evening." He could see Emory was dying to ask him about Maia, but he simply grinned at her and said goodbye.

Atom got into his car and took a beat to breathe. This was it; this was the moment. Don't blow it. He smiled to himself and started the car.

Maia tried not to panic as she parked the car and went into her home. Greeting Betty quickly, she raced upstairs and stripped the bed, putting on fresh sheets, then threw herself into the shower. She dried herself quickly, glancing at the clock. Would he call her bluff and come to see her?

God, she hoped so. It had been a risk, a spur of the moment challenge, but all throughout dinner, she had cast glances at Atom, and knew she wanted him: that dark hair, wild curls around his head, those brilliant green eyes and the shabby, weary look in them… she'd heard the term 'sex on legs' before but had never seen anyone who fit it more than Atom Harcourt. Just his presence sent thrills flooding through her body, and she remembered how she'd first met him, all that time ago. And the fact he'd been the guy at the club... She'd recognized his low, deep sexy-as-hell voice as soon as Emory had introduced them, had seen the curve of his sensual mouth and the dimple in his chin. Right then and there, she knew this was serendipity.

So, she'd made a decision. Fuck the game, she wanted him, and she could tell, just by the way he looked at her, that he wanted her.

Maia just hoped her courage wouldn't fail. She slipped into a light silk robe and brushed out her hair. She heard a car pull up outside and her adrenaline spiked. "Don't be a coward," she whispered to her reflection in the mirror, and put down her brush.

She walked downstairs and opened the door. Atom smiled at her. "Hello again."

All her nerves disappeared, and she went into his arms, her lips seeking his. Atom bent his head to kiss her, his fingers sliding into her hair, pulling her close. The kiss made Maia's head spin and when they finally broke apart, she took Atom's hand and led him inside.

Chapter Eight

There was no question of small talk. They went to her bedroom, and Atom drew her close. "I'm only going to ask this once, my sweet Maia. Are you sure?"
Maia's gaze was steady on his. "More than anything."
Atom stroked her cheek, seeming to take in every detail of her face, his gorgeous green eyes intense and filled with desire. Slowly, he hooked a finger in the belt of her robe and pulled it open, letting the silky gown fall apart. Maia thrilled at the intake of breath he gave when he saw her naked body.
Atom dropped to his knees and buried his face her belly, kissing the soft curve of it. Maia stroked his dark curls with her fingers, then gasped as he pushed her legs apart and his mouth found her clit.
The feel of his tongue on her made her head swim with pleasure, and when he pushed her gently on the bed and

continued to lick, suck, and caress her, Maia felt an orgasm build quickly.

She shivered through it as Atom stripped his shirt off and covered her body. "Hey, beautiful."

Maia felt breathless, her skin covered in a fine sheen of sweat already. She cradled his face in her hands. "Atom…"

He kissed her again hungrily, and Maia reached down to free his straining cock from his pants. God, he was huge, but Maia felt herself grow wet at the thought of it inside her. She moved down the bed to take his cock in her mouth, trailing her tongue up and down the long, thick shaft, enjoying the salty taste of him.

Before he could come, though, he lifted her up so he could kiss her mouth. Reaching to pluck a condom from his abandoned jeans, Atom handed it to her, and she helped him roll it down onto his cock and then he was hitching her legs around his waist.

For a moment, he paused, looking deep into her eyes, then he thrust into her. Maia gasped at the feel of his strong, big cock inside her, but it was a cry of pure ecstasy as they began to move together. It felt like coming home, and Maia knew then she had made the absolute right decision.

Atom made love to her, caressing her body, murmuring her name over and over, his lips trailing across her skin. Maia's fingertips stroked up and down his back, feeling the hard musculature, the smooth olive-shaded skin. She couldn't get enough of his beautiful face, and his eyes,

God, those green eyes, ringed with thick, black lashes… she lost herself in them.

Maia moaned as her orgasm built and built, her entire body on fire, every cell responding to this beautiful man making love to her. Her back arched up, her belly against his as she came, her head flung back, her eyes closing as she came hard, feeling him tense and orgasm just as she did.

Breathless, they gazed at each other while they came down from the high, then both of them laughed. "If you don't mind me saying," Atom panted for air, "I've been waiting a long time for that."

Maia flushed with pleasure, grinning. "I don't mind you saying that at all." She placed her palm on his chest, almost disbelieving that he was here in her bed. "I remember that Christmas party and meeting you on the balcony. I thought you were the most beautiful man I had ever seen, and yet you seemed… lost. I dreamed about you that night."

"You did?"

Maia nodded. "I felt guilty, because I was married then, and at that time, I did love my husband." She swallowed, looking away from his gaze. "But I felt that connection. I just figured it was one of those moments, the lightning bolt moments that were only real in the movies." She looked back at him. "I know now I was wrong."

Atom kissed her, tracing the back of his hand down her cheek. "I'd like to get to know you better, Maia. I'd like the chance to… God, do people still use the word 'court'?"

Maia grinned. "I'm sure we can go for ice cream sodas, Grandpa."

"Ouch." Atom chuckled. "But I'm serious. I know this—" he drew his hand down her body, "—is hardly us being restrained, but I do want to get to know you properly, Maia Gahanna. Twice now you enchanted me—three times—and I want more. Does that scare you?"

Maia studied him, considering. "Before I answer that, can I ask you something?"

"Sure."

"Do you still go to the sex club? And why would you, of all people, need to have anonymous sex? You could have anyone."

Atom nodded. "That's fair." He sat back. "The truth is… I didn't want to find anyone. I didn't want to have a relationship." He was silent for a moment. "My family… my father passed recently. He and I didn't have the best relationship."

"You didn't get along?"

"No. I was never enough for him. My mother was never enough for him. Their marriage was combative. A lot of fights."

Maia slid her fingers through his. "Not the best example to set." She had the feeling there was something else to the story but didn't want to press him. Atom smiled at her, and she noticed how tired he looked. She wrapped her arm around his waist and laid her head on his chest. "I'm sorry you had to go through that."

Atom stroked her hair. "And I'm sorry about your husband."

"I didn't know who he was in the end. To take my daughter with him… I won't ever forgive him for that."
"Tell me about her."
Maia smiled up at him. "You really want to know?"
"I do."
And so, she told him about Luka, and found that with Atom, talking about her beloved Nugget made the pain a bit less, that she could look back with love instead on her daughter. Atom held her while they talked.
The night gave way to dawn and Saturday brought rain. Maia listened to the water hitting the window. They'd talked until the early hours, and she'd asked him to stay. He hadn't hesitated. Now, she lay wrapped in his arms, his lips against the back of her neck, Maia felt something she hadn't had for years. Contentment.
She knew it wouldn't last, that this night had been a fairy tale, but for now, she just enjoyed the feel of his big body next to hers. She turned in his arms, and he opened his eyes and smiled. "Good morning."
"Good morning."
"You're so beautiful," Atom pressed his lips against hers, then grinned apologetically. "Sorry about my morning breath."
"Ha, ditto. I have a spare toothbrush."
He followed her into the small ensuite bathroom, and they brushed their teeth, standing at the sink together. Maia pulled him into the shower, and together they soaped each other's skin, laughing and joking around. They made love again on the bathroom floor before dressing and Maia offered to cook breakfast for him.

"Just coffee will be fine," Atom said, stroking a hand down her back.

Maia smiled. "Good, I'm not a huge breakfast person, either."

Outside, the fall leaves were a glorious riot of colors, and they sat out on her porch swing, ignoring the bite of cold in the air. Atom put his arm around her shoulders, pressing his lips against her temple. "This is a peaceful street."

"It is. Do you live in the city?"

"Mostly, although I've rented a place here while I work on the Harper's house."

Maia nodded. "Emory's been so sweet to me."

"She's a sweetheart alright. Dante's a lucky man. To tell the truth, I owe them. This project, their new home, it's given me back some of my old passion for building homes, for designing them. My company grew so quickly—and I'm not bragging—but it grew so quickly, that almost straight away, I moved away from doing the thing I love—being an architect."

Maia smiled up at him. "So now you're getting back to basics?"

"More like concentrating on the things that matter to me. Like trying to have more meaningful relationships with any remaining, distant family, with my friends… with you, I hope."

Maia leaned her forehead against his. "I like the sound of that." She sighed and checked her watch. "And I hate to do this, but I have a bookstore to open."

"Can I drive you?"

"It's okay, I have my car… but if you're free later, I'd like to cook supper for you."

Atom kissed her. "You have a deal, beautiful. I'll bring the wine."

Lark squinted at her boss as she opened the bookstore. "You look different."

"Do I?" Maia was all innocence but when, a half hour later, her phone beeped with a message from Atom, she couldn't hide her smile. Lark pointed at her, her mouth gaping.

"You hooked up!"

Maia rolled her eyes but couldn't help grinning. "Maybe I did, maybe I didn't."

Lark did a little dance around the store, making Maia laugh, but stopped when a few customers entered the store. Lark slipped behind the register with Maia. "So, who?"

Maia cut her eyes to the customers, and Lark nodded. "Fine," she said, "but as soon as we're alone… details." But the store was busy all that day with people enjoying the autumn day. Both Maia and Lark were busy helping the customers, chatting with them, and while Lark was settled in the children's corner, storytelling, Maia was at the register, handling purchases.

She looked up as a middle-aged man, heavily bearded, came into the shop. She didn't recognize him but that wasn't anything unusual. New customers appeared every day and this man was unremarkable.

It was only when he brought his purchase to the desk that Maia felt a pang. A children's book—A Wrinkle in Time by Madeleine L'Engle.

It had been Luka's favorite. Maia pushed back the spike of pain that shot through her and gave the man a smile. "A good choice. For someone special?"

"My daughter." The man was unsmiling and his tone abrupt and clipped. He had the blackest eyes she had ever seen behind thick glasses. There was something creepy about the way he looked at her. His beard was jet black, his hair, under a flat cap, the same color and Maia noticed now that it seemed off.

"Well, I hope she enjoys it."

She heard the bell on the door jingle and looked around him toward the entrance, eager for the man to leave. She smiled when she saw that Atom was walking through the door. She forgot about the creepy guy, who turned and stalked out as she went to greet Atom.

Atom touched a finger to her cheek, and she smiled. She loved that he was respectful enough not to kiss her in public yet, that he would wait to see how their relationship developed, and how she would approach telling her friends and coworkers about him.

"I'm playing hooky," he explained, "just for a few moments. I had to come to Main Street for some paint swatches."

"Paint swatches already, hey?" Maia stuck her tongue in her cheek. "Man, you build houses real fast."

Atom grinned sheepishly, "Yeah, that was a poor excuse, you got me. I just wanted to see you, but while I'm in town, I'll pick up the wine for later."

Maia flushed with pleasure, and she nodded over to a quieter area of the store, away from Lark's curious stare. "Listen… I feel a little odd saying this, but I want to be honest from the start."

"Uh oh." But he was grinning, and she chuckled. "Nothing bad, I swear… I just… I liked waking up with you this morning."

Atom touched her face again. "Why, Ms. Gahanna, are you asking me to spend the night again? How very modern of you."

She crossed her eyes and poked out her tongue. "If you're lucky, I'll show you an ankle."

"Hussy."

Maia giggled—it felt so good to laugh with him. "By the way, I'm not exactly Ina Garten, but I make a mean lasagna. Good enough?"

"My mother was Italian," he grinned, and she groaned. "Ah, no fair!"

He laughed, throwing his head back. "But she was a terrible cook, and if she were here, she'd tell you the same."

"Oh, you kidder." She prodded his side, and he ducked away, laughing. "You are trouble, Atom Harcourt."

"Your kind of trouble?" His eyes were soft on hers, and at the moment, as far as Maia was concerned, no one else existed in the world.

"Oh, yes," she said, "you're exactly my kind of trouble."

Chapter Nine

Maia curved her back upwards, turning her head so her lips could meet Atom's as he took her from behind, legs pushing hers apart as his cock thrust into her. His hand was splayed on her belly and Maia felt the abandon of someone being thoroughly and professionally fucked. She knew she would never get tired of this, and over the last few weeks, making love with Atom had become almost an addiction. They even made love in the bookstore after closing one night, Atom tumbling her to the floor as they both laughed and joked around.
And every day since, they'd woken up together, neither feeling crowded nor that their relationship was going too fast. They talked about everything, Maia even sharing her pain over Luka and tales of her relationship with Zach. Her relationship with Atom was so different; it felt…
"equal," she told him one night over dinner. "With Zach, there was always the feeling that he was the one in

charge, that I had no agency, and I, being young and naïve, thought that was what marriage or a relationship was."

"Was he ever abusive?"

Maia shook her head. "No, looking back, it was more like he was controlling under the guise of…" She faltered then shrugged. "Of what? I now realize I had no idea who the man was."

"Do you miss him?"

"No." This time she didn't hesitate. "No, not at all. I was twenty-one when I married him. He was my first." She chewed her lip. "I guess I just got caught up in everything. Love bombing—that's a good word for it. He was full-on, all the time." She unconsciously touched her throat. "Looking back now, I felt suffocated, but I didn't know anything else."

Atom stroked her cheek. "We've been spending a lot of time together. I hope you don't feel that way now."

"I don't. Quite the opposite."

They smiled at each other, linking their fingers. "It's strange, but this—us—it's like I've known you for years, but at the same time, I've barely scratched the surface." He leaned forward and kissed her. "And I can't wait to find out what's next."

So now, as they made love on a sleepy Sunday afternoon, three days before Halloween, Maia knew in her heart that she was finally finding peace. Her relationship with Atom was fun, sensual, and she found that she was laughing every day now. Joy had seemed such a stranger for so long.

After Atom had made her come, they lay together talking and joking around. Betty, who knew to keep her distance while they were being intimate, jumped onto the bed and curled up between them.

Maia smiled as Atom kissed the dog's silky head. "She really is a little cutie."

"A home isn't a home without a dog."

"I agree." Atom kissed Maia's mouth. "I have to say, I always thought I was a city guy, but spending all this time out here on the island… it's a whole different way of life." He smoothed Maia's hair back from her face. "Even though I've lived here most of my life, I haven't really even explored the other islands. Have you?"

"I've been to Vashon and Whidbey but only briefly."

"We should go explore together."

Maia smiled at him. "I'd like that." She glanced over at the clock. "Hey, if we're going to make supper with Em and Dante, we'd better get ready."

It was so natural between them, Maia mused as they dressed to go out. A lot of Atom's clothes had migrated here over the past weeks, just from necessity, and his wash bag was a permanent presence in her bathroom. Every day after work, he would come over, and she would have already prepared supper for both of them. Maia chewed her lip now. There was something she had been considering for the last few days, but it would radically change their relationship and after only a few weeks, was it too soon?

Remember your new mantra… take the leap.

"Atom?"

He looked up and gave her that devastating smile. "Yeah, babe?"

Maia swallowed hard and tried to keep the nervous quiver out of her voice. "It seems ridiculous you're paying rent on a house you never use." She took a deep breath. "Why don't you… I mean, if it's not too soon, and if you want, it could be just for while you're working on the Harper house…" She was rambling now and faltered. Atom's smile widened, and he came to her, cupping her cheek in his warm palm.

"Maia, I can't think of anything else I'd like better than to move in here with you. I've practically taken over as it were. But, yes, let's make this official, shall we?" He pressed his lips to hers. "You and Betty are my family now."

Maia's heart swelled up, not least because he included her beloved dog. "I'm so glad."

"One condition. I pay the rent."

"Uh-uh." Maia shook her head. "The most I'll agree to is halfsies."

Atom chuckled. "I knew that, but I thought I'd try. I respect that, babe." He stroked her face. "This isn't just a relationship, this is a partnership. Always. There's no controlling presence in this, not ever. Just reciprocity. I wish that for you above all else—except for one thing."

"What's the one thing?"

His eyes were serious now. "That you could see Luka again."

In that second—that split second—Maia knew she was in love with Atom Harcourt.

Emory kept shooting excited glances at Maia and Atom throughout dinner and afterward, when Maia volunteered to help her with the dessert, the two women went to the kitchen. Maia laughed at Emory's eager expression. "Just ask whatever it is you're wondering, Em."

Emory giggled. "Sorry. It's just so wonderful! You two are adorable together."

"We are, aren't we?" Maia couldn't help laughing then. "He's just the most wonderful man… I can't believe he was single for so long."

Emory nodded, glancing at the door to see if the men could hear them. "Between you and me… he was pretty messed up by his parents. His father—and this is according to Dante—his father was a bastard, a weak man who couldn't express his emotions, and Atom's mother had mental health issues. Not that it was her fault, but she knew and refused to get help for them, even if it meant her own son suffering the consequences."

Maia made a disgusted sound, and Emory nodded. "Quite." She shook her head. "I just don't get it… these people that treat their kids so cavalierly. They just don't get it."

Maia nodded. "Talking of… where's Nella this evening?"

Emory's lovely face broke into a smile. "At a sleepover. Which reminds me… Halloween night. Nella wanted to ask you herself, but she was too shy."

"Go for it."

"She wanted to know if you would go trick or treating with her. She said—and I hope this doesn't upset you—that she was sad you couldn't take Luka trick or treating, and she wanted you to experience what it was like to go with a child."

Maia's heart thumped, both with sadness and with love for the sweet young Nella. "That's beautiful, Em." Her voice got choked, and she had to swallow the lump in her throat. "Tell Nella I would love to. In fact, why don't we make it an occasion? I'll open the bookstore for hot drinks and pumpkin pie, and we'll go out from there?"

Emory high-fived her. "It's a date."

In the car on the way home, Maia told Atom how moved she was by Nella's request. "She's such an adorable kid… and she's the same age as Luka would have been now." She put her hand on her chest. "Oh, God, sorry, I think I'm about to cry."

Atom chuckled and reached for her hand with his free one. "Baby… go ahead and cry all you want."

A few tears came out, but the love she felt from Atom, from Emory and Dante, from Nella conquered any sadness.

They pulled up to her house and Maia frowned. "Didn't we leave the porch light on?"

They got out as they moved closer, Maia gave a gasp of horror. "The door is open."

She darted towards it, and Atom caught her just as she was about to race up the stairs. "Wait, baby. There could be someone in there."

Maia felt panic. "Betty…" The dog wasn't rushing out to meet them, and Maia was filled with a dread. "Betty!"

Atom tucked Maia behind him as he advanced up the stairs. He reached inside the open door and flipped the light on. They both listened for any sound, but there was none—at first.

Then with a sigh of relief, they heard a whine coming from behind the closed kitchen door. Atom went to it and opened it and Betty shot out, greeting them excitedly. Maia felt the tension drain out of her when she saw Betty wasn't hurt. She picked up the dog and hugged her close, following Atom as he checked out every room. He paused as he reached the stairs to the second floor.

"Wait down here, sweetheart. If I yell, get out of the house, into the car and lock the doors. Call the police. Okay?"

Maia nodded, her eyes wide and frightened. She listened as Atom took the stairs two at a time and checked out the second floor. Moments passed.

"All clear, baby." He appeared at the top of the stairs, his relieved smile mirroring hers. Maia put Betty down, and the dog immediately went to the door, scratching to be let out. "She needs to pee." Maia went out with Betty into the front yard. The street was quiet and a faint breeze blew through the trees, rustling the leaves. Maia could hear Atom in the house, checking the windows. She must have left the door open when they left—dumb mistake to make even on a safe street like this.

Betty peed and then sniffed around, and as Maia watched her dog, she noticed a piece of paper fluttering, stuck in the fence. She went over and plucked it out and froze.

It was a photograph of Luka. "What the actual hell?" She murmured to herself. She looked up and around, not really knowing what or who she was looking for, but her shock discombobulated her.

A movement far across the street, in a bank of trees caught her eye, and a shiver went up her spine.

Someone was watching her.

Chapter Ten

Maia waited for Atom to come back and when she heard his knock, she let him in. "No one there, sweetheart."
She sighed. "I'm sorry, you must think I'm paranoid. It's just…" She held up the photograph of Luka. "How the hell did this get outside?"
"Where was it in the house?"
She thought about it. "I think it was lying on a stack on the table in the living room."
"It must have blown out when the door was open."
She nodded. "That's the only explanation." The only non-creepy one at least. She touched the photograph. "It's one of my favorites. I'd put it with some others to frame. For so long I couldn't even bear to look at pictures of her."
Atom smoothed his hand down her hair. "I think that's a great idea. I could make you a frame."
"You could?"

He smiled, nodded. "I studied carpentry as an elective. I love to make things."

"You are the most unusual billionaire, Atom Harcourt." She stood and kissed him. "Let's go to bed."

Maia didn't know what woke her in the night but as she sat up, careful not to wake Atom, tensed and listening to everything in the home. Betty was asleep at the end of the bed, but she opened her eyes and looked up as Maia slipped from the bed. Maia stroke her silky head. "Stay, Betty Boo," she whispered, and the dog licked her hand and settled back down. Maia went down to the kitchen and grabbed a glass. She filled it from the cold faucet and drank it down. Outside, the night was moonless and pitch dark, and she stared out of the window, focusing past her own reflection.

She started when she felt his arms slide around her waist and his lips on the back of her neck. Atom turned her gently to face him, a sleepy smile on his face. Maia pressed her lips to his, and he lifted her into his arms and carried her to the kitchen table, sitting her down. Maia hooked her arms around his neck, pulling his head down so she could kiss him.

His tongue was insistent on hers, but then he drew away, pushing her back onto the table and onto her back. He pulled open her robe and bent to kiss her throat and her breasts, and Maia sighed happily as his lips trailed down her stomach and over the curve of her belly.

They had no need for words now. Atom's cock slid into her, and they began to make love slowly, drinking each other in. The little light there was made the whole scene ethereal, the silence of the night punctured only by their gasps and moans.

Afterwards, he carried her back up to bed, and they wrapped themselves around each other and slept until Maia's alarm clock woke them.

Maia hid her yawn behind her hand, but Lark grinned at her. "Saw that."

"Sorry, I was up late."

Lark snickered. "I bet."

Maia grinned but didn't respond. They were decorating the bookstore's window with more fake spiders' webs. Maia had put a poster in the window announcing the bookstore would be open for warm spiced apple juice and pumpkin pie the following day, and that any parents wanting to bring their kids to trick or treat were welcome to base themselves there.

After lunch, Maia drove to the farmer's market and stocked up on locally made candy and sweets to hand out, throwing in some grapes and apple slices to make little baggies to give out. She thought she should at least make it look a little like she was encouraging healthy eating although she had no doubt the kids would ignore them.

At the check-out, a magazine caught her eye. A small headline, low on the cover of the national publication. Five Years Later—the Mysterious Disappearance of Zachary Konta.

Oh, God damn it. Maia shoved the magazine onto her pile of groceries and didn't meet the cashier's eyes even though she knew there was no way the young girl would make the link.

But paranoid now, Maia went back to her car and sat in the parking lot, flicking to the article. She braced herself for a photograph of Luka but found instead just a small photograph of herself and Zach. She hardly recognized herself in the photo. The biggest picture, though, was the posed and professionally shot photograph of Tracey Golding-Hamm, her beautiful thin face in repose.

Maia nearly gagged when she read the timbre of the piece. Tracey was mourning the loss of her true soulmate, telling the writer that she and Zach shared a 'special bond', that she, if no one else, still wanted to know the truth.

"Others, including his wife, have moved on, healed. My heart, my life will never be the same. It's a shame he wasn't as loved in life as he still is, by me, in death."

"Oh, go fuck yourself, Tracey, you bitch on wheels." Maia was incensed. What a dick move but then why was she surprised?

Atom was at the bookstore when she got back. He rocked back when he saw her expression. "Uh-oh, what's up?"

Maia handed him the article, watched him as he read it. Atom's eyebrows shot up. "Wow. What a piece of work."

"Right?" Maia smiled humorlessly. "Notice she didn't use my name once?"

"I did." Atom looked at the picture of her and Zach and traced her face with his finger tip. "Can I say something?"
"Of course." She sat down next to him, her anger dissipating now. Who cared what Tracey did? That life was a million miles away from her now.
Atom smiled at her. "I don't recognize you in that picture. You look somehow... what's the right word? Caged."
As he said it, Maia realized he was exactly right—exactly right. Zachary Konta had decided he wanted her and had put her into a cage of sorts. Every decision was his and as a feminist, now Maia felt shame. Why hadn't she seen it? Why hadn't she stood up for herself?
"You okay?" There was a crease between Atom's eyebrows as he frowned at her, concerned, and she smoothed it away with her finger.
"I'm fine. That's not my life now."
Atom leaned his forehead against hers. "You're damn straight, it isn't. Our life together will always be happy, I promise you that."
She smiled softly. "Our life."
"You got it, beautiful."

The article put to the back of her mind, Maia concentrated on the joy that her life now brought her. As the trick or treaters began to fill the shop, and the scent of cinnamon and pumpkin spice drifted around, she smiled at both the customers and her friends—her family now. Unique and her girls had come along bearing vast tins of food that Unique had prepared for the event, a surprise for Maia, which almost made her cry. She introduced Emory and Dante to Unique, and Nella was enchanted by the twin girls and their loud, exuberant personalities.

Later, when it was dark, they all went out onto the streets to trick or treat. Nella held Maia's hand the whole time, chatting away excitedly to her 'aunt', and Maia felt something inside her shift. She glanced at Atom who was walking with them, and he smiled at her. Maia had the strangest feeling he was reading her mind, especially when he gave her a small nod. Did he really know what she was thinking? That she would love a child with him? Because she did. So, so badly. It was crazy, yes, but in her heart, she knew it was her destiny to make a family with this incredible man.

At the final house, Nella hit pay dirt, and crowed delightedly to everyone in ear shot. Emory and Dante teased their daughter as Maia took out her phone to snap a picture of them all.

As they posed, and Maia stepped away from the group toward the edge of the sidewalk, Nella suddenly ran over to her, slipped and tumbled into the road. In a heartbeat everything changed. The car coming at them didn't stop, and as Maia scooped a crying Nella up, she lost her own balance. She shoved Nella into her mother's arms as she fell and bounced spectacularly off of the car's hood. Time seemed to stop as she was spun in the air, hearing screams around her, then she crashed to the cold, hard asphalt, and everything went dark.

Chapter Eleven

Maia pushed the nurse's hands away and struggled into a sitting position. "I'm really fine."
Atom rolled his eyes as the nurse pursed her lips. "Maybe so, Ms. Gahanna, but until the doctor clears you, you need to stay in bed."
Maia sighed but gave in. Her body ached like hell, but thankfully, there were no broken bones. Maia was more worried about Nella, but when a pale, shaken Emory assured her that Nella was unhurt, just worried about her 'aunt', Maia was relieved.
Atom took her hand, wincing when he saw the cuts on it. She had multiple contusions, cuts, and her face felt swollen. She dared not look at her reflection.
The doctor came at last and told her he'd prefer if she stayed in overnight to be sure, but that there were no head injuries to be concerned about. "You might have a slight concussion, and obviously you'll ache for a while.

Take aspirin for the pain, maybe some ibuprofen, too. You'll be fine."

"I would prefer not to stay the night."

"She'll stay the night," Atom said firmly, but when Maia glared at him, he seemed to realized he was breaking his promise to her. "Of course, it's not my decision."

"Right."

Atom squeezed her hand in apology as Maia looked back at the doctor. "Seriously, I'd rather go home."

"I don't see any harm in that. Just rest for a few days, please, and if you feel worse, come right on back." He smiled at them and left them alone.

Atom sat next to Maia on the bed and kissed her temple. "I'm sorry, baby. You just scared the crap out of me. And that asshole didn't even stop."

Maia shrugged. "These things happen. I just want to go home, take a bath and go to bed… with you." She wiggled her eyebrows at him and he laughed.

"Ambitious, but I somehow don't think we'll be doing anything but sleeping tonight."

Maia grumbled, but it turned out he was right. After a hot soak in the tub, she fell asleep almost immediately.

Atom lay beside her until he was sure she was completely out, then got up. Betty immediately took his place next to Maia, and Atom grinned at the dog. "You keep her safe and warm, Betty Boo."

He went downstairs and closed the kitchen door behind him. He called Dante. "How's Nella?"

"She's fine. We plied her with sweets and cake, and she stayed up way past her bedtime, but she's out now. Em's just checking on her. How's Maia?"

"Bruised, battered, but she'll be okay." Atom took a deep breath in. "Dante... you saw that car."

"It drove right at her."

Atom nodded to himself. "It wasn't an accident, was it?"

"I don't think so. Listen, I spoke to the detective, told them everything. They don't hold out hope the car will be found—there are not a lot of security cameras on that particular street. Something tells me the driver knew that."

Atom felt his heart sink. "Who, though? Who the hell would want to hurt Maia?"

Dante was silent for a moment, then sighed. "I know all about vengeful exes, Atom."

"God. You really think this is Konta?" Atom rubbed his head.

"He was—or is—not a good guy, Atom. He had a lot of people fooled for a long time. You have people in Manhattan?"

"Three or four private hires. They've not come up with anything so far, no sign of him. If he is out there somewhere with Maia's daughter... he's well hidden."

"We know he was syphoning off money from his company for years. He has unlimited funds to hide forever if that's his game. Except... why would he risk it all now, to come back for Maia?"

Atom let out a deep, ragged breath. "Because she's happy. From what I know of narcissists, he won't let her be happy without him."

Another silence. "Atom… your mom…"

"We don't need to talk about her, but yes. Yes."

He ended the call to Dante and sat in the dark kitchen for a while, thinking. He hated that he was going behind Maia's back to snoop into her past, but if there was one thing that Atom wanted more than anything, it was to give Maia a final answer. Was Luka alive?

And why the hell would Zach Konta do this to the wife he professed to love? Atom thought he knew the answer to that, but it meant him thinking about his own experiences…… and he wasn't ready for that. And he wouldn't lay that burden on Maia. No. He would protect her all he could while they were trying to find out where Konta had hidden himself.

Because Atom would bet his life that he was alive. He could only hope that somewhere, Luka was alive, too.

He went back to the bedroom and lay down next to Maia and Betty. Betty stirred and sleepily snuffled at him. He stroked the dog's head, then tucked a lock of Maia's dark hair away from her face. There was a nasty bruise on her cheek, a cut over her eye but to him, she looked more beautiful than anything. In the few weeks they had been together, Atom had finally learned what a true partnership was. Fun, laughter, truth, as well as the incredible sex. Now he truly knew what the term soulmate meant, and he was damned if anyone—anyone—was going to ruin their love.

Love. Atom chuckled softly to himself. For most of his life, he hadn't known what that meant. The love he had was from his friends, not his family, and now…

"I love you," he whispered to her, wishing he had the courage to say it when she could hear him. "I love you so very much, Maia Gahanna."

He leaned over and kissed her lips gently, so gently that he knew he wouldn't wake her. He wrapped his arm around her waist and closed his eyes. Tonight had been a nightmare; Atom could still feel the sheer horror and the panic he'd experienced when the car had hit Maia. Her little body flying through the air. Her crumpled body on the asphalt, bloodied and broken. He'd thought she was dead.

God.

Atom vowed then it would be the worst thing he would ever let happen to her. Not again, he thought. Not ever again.

He'd dumped the car, cleaned it of all trace of himself. He switched the license plates, just to be sure, but he was confident they wouldn't be able to trace him, even if they had his DNA on file.

She'd probably given his DNA to them after he'd gone missing five years ago. He supposed it was meant to be so touching, the way she had looked for him all those years: the pleas on television and in the papers, the hiring of the private investigators. All of it a lie—her concern, her worry false.

Whore.

If only you had been so true when we were married, my love. It had displeased him when she had divorced him, but he could understand her anger. He'd taken her most precious thing—Luka.

And now, after all of that, she had moved on with Atom Harcourt, that fucked-up piece of shit. Had Atom told her all about his past? He'd found out about Harcourt and what had happened to him after he'd seen the man flirting with Maia on the balcony at Henry's party. True, they had only spoken a few words, but he had been in shadows, watching them.

He knew an instant connection when he saw it. He had almost been on the cusp of changing his mind about what he was going to do, but seeing them together, seeing that man dare to smile, to touch what was his…

He'd known then they were fucking and now she'd taken their relationship public. The grieving widow finds love again. Ah, how fucking sweet.

Zach Konta had two choices back then. Kill her or do what he did—take him and his daughter out of the loop. He chose the second option, but now he was rethinking that choice. Because she was fucking Atom Harcourt, because she had moved on from him.

Because she was happy.

Not for much longer, my love. But first, he would make her suffer like no one had ever suffered before.

He knew that before he killed her, before he felt her blood on his hands, he, Zachary Konta, would send his beautiful ex-wife to Hell…

Chapter Twelve

It took a few weeks for her body to return to normal and even then, she still ached. "I guess the bruises went deeper than I realized," she said to Atom one day. They had healed, but it felt like some were bone deep, and belatedly she wondered if she were slipping back into depression.
The difference this time was she could talk to her partner in life about it. Atom listened to her without judgement and suggested she talk to a therapist or see a doctor. "There's no shame in asking for help, baby."
She was more grateful to him that she could express. God, this man…
It was almost Thanksgiving, and Maia had invited the Harpers and the Benjamins to her place for the traditional meal. Lark was with her family but said she would stop by later in the day for mulled wine and pumpkin pie.

Atom had taken the day before Thanksgiving off to help her prepare the house—their house now. He had moved in the day after she asked him to and since then, they had fallen in love with the place, so much so that Atom had approached the owner to see if he would sell it to them. Maia had been surprised. "Don't you want somewhere grander?"

Atom had shaken his head. "No, I really don't. This place is plenty big for us and Betty—for our kids."

It was strange how quickly they had gotten used to the idea that yes, this was it for both of them. They had found their person.

And now they had something else to celebrate, something they would tell their friends about over dinner. Maia grinned to herself now as she prepared the stuffing for the turkey. She could hardly believe it herself.

She thought back now to when they had decided to do 'the crazy thing'. A few days after her accident, she had gone out onto the porch to find Atom sitting pensively on the swing seat. She sat down next to him, smoothing his dark curls away from his face. "Are you okay?"

He turned to her, a warm smile spreading across his gorgeous features, and she saw raw, pure emotion in his eyes. "I am. I am, baby, I think for the first time in forever. I'm changing, Maia, and it's only for the better."

"I don't see how you could get much better," she joked but, grinning, he shook his head.

"There're things… things that I've never shared with anyone. Stuff from my childhood. My parents… they were not good people, and I've been so scared that I would turn out the same."

"Not a chance." She kissed his cheek. Atom wrapped his arms around her.

"I hoped not, but it's hard to see yourself clearly. Things get warped. But being with you… if I were that bad, you wouldn't be with me."

"You are not bad, Atom. Not even a single cell in your body is bad. You are the most wonderful person I've ever met. You are kind, considerate, funny, and sexy as hell. The full package." She stroked his face, her eyes steady on his. "And I love you."

His smile was delighted. "As I love you, my darling, my beautiful Maia, so very much."

They kissed and soon Maia had taken his hand and led him inside and upstairs to bed.

Maia smiled now. Neither of them had slept that night, knowing it was a significant moment in their lives, their relationship. They talked and made love and planned their future and since then, they had grown closer than ever.

Maia stretched now. All of her cuts and bruises were gone, only a little muscle ache remained. She looked up as Atom returned from the market with the turkey. "Woah Nelly," she said, her eyes boggling at the size of it, "how many people are we feeding?"

Atom grinned. "Well, there's the eight of us… and then there's…" He nodded to Betty, who sat between them, her eyes riveted to the uncooked turkey. "She knows…"

Maia laughed. "In that case, you probably should have gotten two." She kissed Atom and ruffled the dog's head. "Patience, Betty Boo, tomorrow will come soon enough." She watched as Atom hefted the turkey onto the table. "Jeez, it is big, though. I think I have a pan to fit it, but it's packed away in the attic."

"Want me to get it?"

"No, I'll go. I might find some other useful stuff up there." She glanced at the clock. "You could give Guts McLagan her supper, though." Betty's ears pricked up despite the nickname.

Atom laughed, and Betty got excited as he moved to where they kept the dog food. "We're so domesticated."

"Aren't we?" Maia chuckled. "I'll be right back."

She pulled down the ladder to the attic and climbed up. It was remarkably light and airy for an attic space, her few boxes she hadn't opened neatly stacked at one end. She sorted through them, found the items she wanted and turned to go back downstairs.

Then she saw it. A small item, almost in darkness at the far end of the attic space. She frowned. She hadn't noticed it before. She walked over, but as she realized what it was, all the breath left her body, she went ice cold and her legs gave way. She sank to the floor, reaching for the small woolen hat. The blue woolen hat with the pink star on it.

Luka's favorite hat. The hat she had been wearing when she disappeared. Maia couldn't breathe. She opened her mouth to scream and nothing would come out. She clutched the hat to her face, breathing in, trying to see if any of Luka's baby powder scent remained.

Maia closed her eyes. Time stood still, and it wasn't until she felt Atom's arm around her that she looked up at him, tears swimming in her eyes. She held out the hat to him and he took it, turning it over in his hands.

She watched his expression, saw the sympathy, his pain for her in his eyes. "Oh, my darling," he whispered. "I'm so sorry. I wish I could bring her back to you."

Maia shook her head and finally found her voice even if it cracked and broke. "No, you don't understand… I don't know why this is here. It can't be here, it isn't possible… she was wearing this." Her voice rose now, hysterical. "She was wearing this when he killed her…"

Chapter Thirteen

Atom shot a glance at Maia. She was doing an incredible job of hiding how she was really feeling, and none of their friends had picked up on her sadness. Yesterday had been traumatic. They talked for hours, Maia going over everything, doubting her own mind about what Luka had been wearing that terrible day.

It had upset her to think she had misplaced memories of her daughter. "I was so sure. In my mind I've had this picture in my head for five years about what she was wearing the very last time I saw her. To think I was wrong makes me want to scream, Atom."

"Maybe you weren't wrong?" Atom had stroked her hair but Maia, too agitated to be comforted, stood up, walking away from him, pacing the room.

"Then how is it here? How?"

Atom gave her a moment before speaking again. "Darling, perhaps the police returned it to you and you just forgot?"

Maia didn't answer, and he could see she was desperately trying to believe that was the case… because the alternatives were too fucked up to consider. That either she was crazy or someone had put the hat there.

Jesus…

When she'd finally fallen asleep, he'd put a call into his private investigators in New York, not caring that it was five hours ahead, nor that it would be the early hours of the morning there, but none of them had anything to report. Atom then called his own head of security. "I want a discreet—and I mean, discreet—watch on Maia's bookstore. Also, for now… keep your distance, but I want her protected wherever she goes."

"Wherever who goes?"

He turned to see Maia watching him. "I'll call you back," he told his security chief and ended the call. He stood and faced Maia, unable to read her expression. "My security team. I want you protected."

"From whom?" She looked at him askance.

Atom hesitated. This was the moment; he'd have to share his possibly insane theory with her, and worse, it could terrify her. "From the possibility someone means you harm. The accident that might not have been an accident at all. The open door. The hat." He took a deep breath. "The fact that no bodies were ever found."

To his surprise, Maia didn't freak out on him. Instead she sat down heavily next to him. "I've been thinking the same thing. It just seems weird that that Tracey would choose to do that now... and by now, I don't mean the five-year anniversary, I mean, just when I found happiness with you. So, yeah... maybe it is Zach pulling the strings, I wouldn't put it past him."

Atom studied her. "I've had people in New York digging around."

"And?" She didn't seem either pissed or surprised.

"Nothing much except... he wasn't a good guy. Not that we've found any evidence of... anything, but the people we've talked to...very few of them had good things to say."

Maia's expression was stone. "He either killed his daughter or let me believe he did. That's enough for me to believe he's scum." Anger rippled through her voice. "And if he's back to torment me..." Atom saw her hands clench into fists.

"What?"

She looked at him with a steady gaze. "You can't kill a dead man twice."

He should have been shocked, he thought now, but truthfully, there wasn't any doubt in his mind that he would help Maia hide the body if it came to that. But she didn't say anything else, and when morning came, she seemed sheepish.

He'd been shaving when she slid behind him and wrapped her arms around his waist. "You know I was just fronting yesterday, right? I'm not a psycho, I swear."

Atom chuckled. "Baby, I know that. And you have more than enough justification for it. I'd help you hide the body, Boo." But he'd said it in a joking way, and Maia had chuckled.

"That might be the most romantic thing you've ever said to me." She kissed him as he laughed. "Hey, Clyde, wanna come do me in the bedroom?"

"Try and stop me, Bonnie." He chased her into the bedroom, Maia screaming with laughter as he wrestled her to the bed.

All tension seemed gone as they made love, and later that afternoon, as their friends all gathered at their home, Maia seemed perfectly contented, and he was glad of it.

Maia had knocked it out of the park with the Thanksgiving spread, and after the meal, everyone sat around in the living room, groaning at their full bellies. Jamelia lay on her back on the floor, staring up at the ceiling like she was in a stupor. "Jams, are you okay?" Maia grinned down at her.

"Food coma. Mom, I think you have competition."

"Ha." Maia said, flushing, giving Unique a nervous glance. "Believe me, one meal does not make a chef. I bow to you, my queen."

Unique cackled as Maia bowed, waving her hands at her. "Girl, sit down. The meal was amazing, don't sell yourself short. Besides, if I ever need help to cater, I'll be able to ask you."

"If you want drive all your clients away, sure. Atom will tell you, today was a fluke." Maia sat down on Atom's lap, hooking her arm around his neck. "Isn't that right, honey?"

Atom grinned up at her. "Loaded question… all

right, I'm kidding! No, she's a great cook, Unique, one of her many talents."

"Mushy." Emory pretended to gag, then laughed. "So, what is this announcement you were going to make?"

Maia and Atom looked at each other, then both chuckled. "You tell them, baby."

Maia's face burned but she smiled. "Well... we got married."

Her friends' faces were identical with shock. "What?" Emory gaped at them. It took Nella, the ten-year-old, to react first.

"Yay!" She launched herself at Maia and Atom, who laughed and hugged the girl. Then all of their friends were congratulating them, and it took a few minutes for them to calm down.

"So, details?" Michonne said, settling back down in her seat. "When, where, how?"

So, Maia told her. Atom had proposed to her, almost as a joke at first, one evening as they were watching TV on her couch. But the joke had tuned into something more serious—or rather, they started to dare each other to make the leap by making ridiculous bets until they both realized they both wanted it more than anything.

"So, we went to City Hall the next day before we lost our nerve. I'm sorry we didn't tell anyone, but we wanted to get used to the idea first." Atom stroked his hand down Maia's cheek. "We like to say we got married by accident, but it was the best decision I have ever made."

"Right back at you, hubby." She kissed him, then

glanced across at Emory. "Emory Harper, are you crying?"

"No…" But she was. "Sorry, I'm a sucker for a love story. Congratulations, guys. Some people might think it's fast, but you know what? Anyone who saw you together wouldn't think so. Hell, I wish we'd known! We could have brought champagne!"

Atom tipped Maia from his lap, making her giggle. "Just so happens…"

He disappeared into the kitchen and brought back a bottle of champagne, struggling to hang on to the flutes. Maia rescued him and soon they all held their flutes up in a toast. "To Maia and Atom. May your lives be happy, healthy, and full of joy. Congrats, kids." Dante raised his glass, and the others echoed him.

Later, well after midnight, when all their friends had left, Maia and Atom showered together, then went to bed. Atom stroked his hand down her body. "Are you tired, my love?"

"Not for you," she whispered and pressed her lips to his. Atom pulled her on top of him as they kissed, and then Maia sat up, straddling him. His hands spanned her waist as hers stroked his cock until it was rock-hard and trembling.

Maia guided him into her wet warmth, tightening her muscles around him, making him moan as she moved on top. His hands caressed her full breasts, his thumbs stroking a rhythm over her nipples, making them hard and uber-sensitive.

Maia's hair tumbled around her shoulders, and in the moonlight, Atom gazed up at her, wondering at this woman, this incredible woman, who loved him without condition, without taking anything from him.

They fell asleep soon after making love, snuggled together in the bed.

Chapter Fourteen

The nightmare began like it always did: in his childhood home, a vast, cavernous cold mansion he'd always hated. Despite the size of it, he could still hear his mother and father screaming at each other, each barbed attack more vicious, more hateful. How, how could he be related to these monsters?
He would hide. As a kid, and even now, as a grown man, the imperative was to run, run far away, get out, hide. But in the nightmare, there was no escape. The walls were solid, grey stone and every door he closed melted away as the banshee cries of his mother came closer. She would come to him, desperate to love and be loved but utterly incapable of that feeling. So, she would punish him, again and again, verbally, physically until he was bleeding and broken and begging to die.

And then, one night, she tried to give him his wish. He had fallen asleep after stealing liquor from his father's cabinet. He was fourteen years old and home from boarding school—his only respite—and his physical beauty was beginning to shine. Both boys and girls were entranced by it. His mother was jealous.

He was in a deep sleep, dreamless, when he felt something cold against his chest. He woke to see his mother, nude, straddling him, but she wasn't trying to rape him. Instead, she held a knife in her hand, the tip against his chest, over his heart.

"It's for the best, my darling," she whispered and leaned her weight on the knife. In reality, Atom had thrown her off before the knife could penetrate his heart, and his mother, screaming, had turned the knife on herself and slashed her wrists as Atom staggered from the room. But in the dream, the knife pierced him all the way through, and the pain was searing. Tonight's nightmare was particularly horrifying. As his mother murdered him, he saw a shadowy figure behind her, a man carrying the body of a woman, and he knew without a doubt it was Zachary Konta, carrying Maia's dead body. As Atom bled out, Konta threw Maia onto him. "Keep her." Konta growled. "You deserve each other." Maia's eyes were open and staring, sightless and clouded, no life to be found anywhere in them.

Atom awoke suddenly, crying and screaming, "No, please, Maia, breathe, live, don't leave me… please…"

It took a moment for him to feel her arms around him, holding him tightly, her warm, soft voice calming and sweet. "It's okay, baby, I'm here, I'm here… I love you, you're safe…"

Adrenaline was pumping through his body, and he collapsed sobbing as Maia held him, knowing he could break down, and she wouldn't judge or mock him for doing so… and God, the years of pent-up rage and hurt and terror came flooding out.

Maia stroked his head, her lips against his temple, letting him get it all out. Finally, as his sobbing subsided, she wiped the tears away from his face. "You needed that, didn't you?"

He nodded. "I'm sorry, I didn't realize that would happen."

"Was it a nightmare? You've had them a few times since we've been together."

Atom was surprised. "You noticed?"

"I have." She smiled at him. "I've wanted to ask you about them before, but I also didn't want you to feel like… I don't know, that I was prying. But… talk to me, darling. There is nothing you can't tell me, my love."

Atom hesitated. "It was so long ago."

"But whatever it is still affects you, so out with it. You know all my dark secrets." She half-smiled. "But I'm serious. You once told me it didn't help to keep it in. We're married now. Tell me."

And so, Atom told her the horrifying story of his teenage years: the fights, the manipulation, ending with the murder attempt and his mother's suicide.

"Of course, my father didn't believe me. He blamed me for her death, didn't believe that she had tried to kill me,

despite my injuries. He thought I'd struggled to get the knife from her, but even that wasn't good enough."
Atom let out a deep breath. "Over the years, he began to accept that Mother had serious mental health issues, but still… we never reconciled."
"Oh, sweetheart, I'm so sorry." Maia wrapped her arms around him. "I can't even imagine."
He kissed her. "I honestly never knew what love was until I met you. I mean, yes, my friends, Dante especially, gave me love, but I could never imagine that I would let someone get so close to me. And I'm still terrified of losing you."
"That, I can promise you, will never, ever happen. Whatever life holds for us now, you and I are a team." Maia kissed him fiercely. "And I love you. I know now you are the only man I have ever loved. You have taught me what love is."
Atom's arms tightened around her, and they began to make love again, shutting out the rest of the world until dawn broke over the island.

Chapter Fifteen

Lark peered at Maia from behind the counter. "Are you all right, boss? You're very quiet today."
"Am I? Sorry, just pondering… stuff. Sorry. Listen, it's dead today. Why don't we shut for an extended lunch—my treat—and we'll go pick up a tree for the shop?"
It was the first week of December, and Maia felt restless as if she were missing… something. Atom's story had unsettled her, but she was careful not to show that around him, wanting to be strong for him. He'd found a therapist in the city and had arranged an appointment for the New Year. There was a renewed life in his eyes, and Maia felt as if a strange unknown weight had been lifted from them.
If only the weight she was feeling was so easy to figure out. The notion that Zach was alive and hunting her… but how the hell had he known where she was? The only answer was that he'd been watching her the whole time,

but that idea made her want to throw up. What kind of sick, twisted mind…

No, she told herself. There are easy answers. The hit-and-run was an accident, the break-in simply a matter of forgetting to lock up after herself, and the hat…

Luka was wearing another hat. A different hat. I just remembered it wrong.

It helped her to think like that, but a small part of her wondered. If Zach was alive… was there a possibility Luka was, too?

Stop it. Don't trust to hope.

Maia glanced at the clock. It was five of noon now and the store was empty. She quickly scribbled a sign and stuck it in the window. "Come on, Larkie. Let's go eat." They had a quick lunch at their favorite sandwich place then went to find a spruce tree. Hefting it into the back of Maia's car, they then went to find decorations for it. They spent an obscene amount of money, which made Lark quell but Maia just laughed. "It's an investment. We'll use these over and over, you'll see."

Back at the store, there was a small queue of people waiting, and Maia apologized to them and offered them all free eggnog or warm spiced apple juice. Soon the bookshop was full of people, some of whom helped decorate the tree as Maia served customers.

Finally, she was able to come join them at the tree, and she strung tiny white lights all over it, jokingly wrapping them around Lark, too.

"I'm sure this counts as employee abuse." The younger woman giggled as Maia looped Christmas balls over each of Lark's ears.

Someone cleared their throat, and the two women turned to see the creepy man from a few weeks ago waiting impatiently at the counter. Maia shot Lark a resigned look and went to serve him.

If anything, he was freakier still, standing way too close to her as she showed him some new children's books they just had delivered. She felt his breath on her shoulder, his musty scent. Yuck, she thought, have a shower once in a while. It was impossible to figure out how old he was; his hair and beard were speckled with grey but the too-black color of his hair suggested he dyed it. His eyes, darker than dark, were riveted to her, unblinking.

Maia felt uncomfortable and moved back to the register, eager to put space between him and herself. She wrapped his books for him and took his money. "Thank you. Have a great holiday season."

She expected him to turn silently and stalk out, but he lingered. "I wonder," he started, again pinpointing her with that unsettling stare. "Would you like to have a drink with me?"

Maia sighed inwardly but smiled politely. "That's very kind but—" she held up her left hand, "—I'm very happily married."

He stared at the simple white gold band on her ring finger for the longest time, until Maia put her hand down, behind her back.

This time, he did turn and stalk out without a word. Maia let out a long breath of relief, her shoulders slumping. Lark, having finally disentangled herself from the lights, came over. "Jeez, that guy is a real piece of work."

"Why do I feel like I need a shower?" Maia shuddered theatrically and laughed. "Ah, who cares? Listen, you've gone above and beyond today. Why don't you skip out early?"

"Are you sure?"

"Of course. Do you need a ride home?"

"No, it's fine, I have my bicycle." Lark wound her scarf around her neck. "Thanks, Maia. I'll see you in the morning."

It was almost closing time by the time Maia had seen to the last customer, and she quickly put back some books before she closed the store. As she slid the last book onto the shelf, she almost groaned when she heard the door open.

Fixing a smile on her face, she went back to the front and stopped. The creep was back. He gave her a smile—or rather, stretched a rictus across his face in an imitation of one.

"I don't easily take no for an answer."

Maia felt both anger and fear surge through her. What the fuck was he thinking? "I'm sorry, but we're closed." She walked to the door and opened it, not backing down for one moment.

"I said I—"

"I heard what you said, sir, but I have already given you my answer. Please leave."

He didn't move. Maia grew impatient. "Look, there's no need for this to be unpleasant. If you think you're intimidating me, you're very much mistaken. Now, please, this store is closing for the evening, and I want to go home to my husband."

They stared at each other for a long moment, neither backing down. Then the door opened a bit more, and a muscular man who Maia vaguely recognized stepped into the store, his eyes riveted to the creep.

"Is there a problem here, Mrs. Harcourt?"

Maia tried not to show her surprise, and in that moment, she realized the newcomer was one of Atom's security team. She hid a grin. "None, thank you. This gentleman was about to leave."

The creep shot a spiteful glance at her but was clearly not going to take on the young man, whose biceps were thicker than Maia's waist. He left silently, and the security guard closed the door behind him. He smiled at Maia. "Sorry if I stepped on your toes. I know you were handling it; I was just back-up."

Maia smiled back at him. "No, thank you, really. That could have gotten nasty and as feminist as I am, I'm not stupid. I would have tried to fight him off, but who knows whether I would have succeeded. Thank you." She realized she was trembling. "Jeez. Listen… let's meet properly. I'm assuming you work for Atom?"

He held out his hand, and she shook it. She liked his calm, easy manner. "Ash Oliver. I'm on Mr. Harcourt's team, yes, but relatively new."

"From Washington?"

"Born and bred, ma'am."

Maia waved her hand. "God, please, it's Maia. 'Ma'am' makes me sound like a grandma. Well, Ash, thank you. I do appreciate it… I have to be honest, I had no idea Atom had assigned protection to me." She vaguely remembered something about protection, but she and Atom had never discussed it again.

"We keep our distance," Ash said now. "The last thing Mr. Harcourt wanted was you to feel watched. But he will want to know about this, sorry."

"It's okay but I'll tell him. We have no secrets. No big secrets." She amended with a grin.

"Do you need a ride home?"

Maia smiled at him. He really was cute with that dirty blonde hair and hazel eyes. "No, I have my car, thank you."

Chapter Sixteen

At home, she began chopping vegetables for their supper, waiting for Atom to come back from the construction site. When she heard his key in the door, she went to meet him. He grinned at her as he hung his coat on the hook. "Hey, beautiful."
In reply, Maia wrapped herself around him, pressing her lips to his and kissing him until they were both breathless. "Wow," he said, "now that's a way to say hello."
"Next you'll be saying 'somethin' smells good' and 'honey, I'm home.'" She grinned at him and he laughed. "We're so domesticated. Talking of… where's the kid?"
"Eating her supper." Maia gave him a guilty look. "Yeah, I know it's early, but she was driving me crazy."
As if on cue, Betty came barreling out of the kitchen to greet Atom, and he swept the dog into his arms. "At least I know where I come on the scale, Betty Boo. After Mommy and your food."

"To be fair, you come after food on my scale, too… no, don't!" She giggled as he lunged for her, tickling her. She escaped his grip and skipped to the kitchen. "Go wash up, it's almost ready."

When he came back down, clean, in a fresh sweater and jeans, he picked the lid of the saucepan up. "Meatballs?" He looked hopeful, and she laughed.

"A man of habits." She pulled herself up onto the counter and studied him. "It's a thank you."

"For what?"

Maia hid a smile. "For giving me Cute-Boy bodyguard."

Atom stopped, raising his eyebrows. "Ash?"

"The very one."

Atom's smile faded. "If you met him, then something happened."

"No biggie. Just an overzealous admirer. I was handling it, but Ash was back-up."

"Nope, tell me everything."

So, keeping her word to Ash, she related everything to Atom, whose face was like stone afterward. "Do you understand what he could have done to you?"

"I'm aware. And I'm not complaining about you protecting me, although, dude, you could have told me." His eyes softened. "I promised not to put you in any kind of cage."

"And this isn't it, Atom. I appreciate it, just next time, tell me in advance. But," she put her hands on his chest, "don't think I'm busting your balls. Like I said, I appreciated the back-up."

Over dinner, she could tell Atom was thinking about the creeper. She nudged his knee with her foot. "Hey. Stop dwelling. You know how often a woman gets harassed by a man?"

"Weekly?"

"Try daily. Sometimes multiple times a day. Sometimes it's something like standing way too close in a check-out line. Might not seem a big deal, but it's someone taking something from us. Anyway, enough about that. How's the house coming along?"

He told her the progress on the Harper house. "Which reminds me… I got a call today from a company I did some work for in New York. They're holding a Christmas party and wondered if I would attend as a special guest." Atom searched her eyes. "What do you think? Are you ready to go back to Manhattan?"

Maia felt a jolt of shock, then considered. She knew there would possibly be some of her old social circle would be there—more of a certainty, really. Was she ready to go back?

Atom took her hand. "No pressure, but it might help. You've told me how some of them treated you. Go back with your head held high, Maia. Fuck 'em."

"You know what? You're right." She took a deep breath in. "Let's do it."

Atom leaned over and kissed her. "I'll make the arrangements."

So, a week before Christmas, Maia and Atom traveled to New York. Atom had booked the penthouse suite of a high-end motel overlooking Central Park, and as they dressed for the party, Maia looked out over the city, over the view she had known for so long. Now, she wondered how she could ever pass up Washington's mountains and oceans for this log-jam of a city.

Atom noticed her reverie and kissed the back of her neck. "You okay?"

She nodded and smiled at him. "Always when I'm with you."

Atom slid an appreciative hand down her dark gold dress which clung to her curves and highlighted her caramel skin. "You look sensational."

She pressed her body against his. "After the party, we're going to keep each other up all night long." She grinned at him, reaching down to cup his cock through his pants and he chuckled.

"You're on, beautiful."

In the cab to the party, she held his hand, nerves creeping into her, and Atom seemed to notice, squeezing her fingers to comfort her. "I'm with you," he whispered, leaning in to kiss her, "always."

At first, she didn't recognize anyone and began to relax a little, but Maia and Atom were early.. She knew that Sakata and Henry would be at the party; she kept in touch with her old friend but hadn't seen her for a couple of years.

Still, as the evening wore on, familiar faces appeared, some who she'd known vaguely, others who had been friends to Zach more than her. Few of them approached her, however, choosing to just stare and gossip. Maia's head went up, and she ignored them—especially those who had been friends with her despised ex-husband. She was proud to stand up with Atom, but as the night wore on, she had to take a time out to regroup. She excused herself and headed to the ladies' restroom. Inside she took a few deep breaths, closing her eyes. Being around these people, especially at this time of the year, was bringing back all kinds of memories, good and bad, but mostly of Zach.

When had she started to hate him? Was it really only after he'd taken Luka from her? Or had it started earlier? Looking back, having now entered into a marriage of equals, of fun and of freedom, she shook her head at how naïve she had been in her first marriage, how sheltered. How restricted. Maia shook her head now and washed her hands. That life is over, she thought, and it helps no one to dwell.

She was leaving the bathroom as the door was pushed open, and she found herself face-to-face with Tracey Golding-Hamm. Maia gave an audible groan and rolled her eyes. "Tracey... what a displeasure."

"Well, if it isn't the grieving widow. Or, seeing as you've managed to capture another rich man in your web, should I say, black widow?"

"Hilarious," Maia shot back. "Listen, I read your sob story... you do realize that, Zach being dead and all, that you lost your chance with him, right? Unless you're up for fucking a murderous corpse."

She didn't care that she was being a bitch, Tracey deserved every bit of vitriol Maia could send her. She saw something flicker in Tracey's eyes then, and a thrill of shock went through her. It wasn't annoyance or hurt… it was triumph. Was Tracey enjoying Maia fighting back for once, or was it something else? Something that Tracey knew and Maia didn't?

Like Zach being alive… Maia opened her mouth to say something, but they were interrupted by a banshee cry of joy and Sakata bore down on them, practically shoving Tracey out of the way and throwing her arms around Maia's neck.

"Maia Gahanna, it's been too damn long." Sakata sounded like she was about to burst into tears, and Maia hugged her friend back tightly as she saw Tracey disappear.

Damn it. But she couldn't stay annoyed because just being with Sakata was heavenly. Sakata dragged her back to the party. "Introduce me to your gorgeous man."

Maia found Atom already chatting with Henry, and she introduced her friend to her new husband. Sakata sized him up blatantly for a long moment, then turned with a serious face to Maia. "Now he, Ms. Gahanna, is a serious, serious upgrade."

They all burst out laughing as Sakata grinned, her gorgeous eyes crinkling at the sides. She and Atom flirted playfully as Maia and Henry chuckled, listening to their back and forth.

Maia saw Tracey again as she and Atom were leaving with Sakata and Henry, and the other woman smirked at her.

Henry was talking so Maia felt she couldn't interrupt to go over and talk to Tracey about what she knew, but it was in the back of her mind for the rest of the evening.

Chapter Seventeen

They were staying in New York for a few more days before going back to Bainbridge Island, and tomorrow, Maia would spend a long, leisurely lunch with Sakata before Christmas shopping with her old friend. Atom had business meetings all day, and Maia thought about how few times she had seen him dress for business rather than in his jeans and T-shirt to work on the Harper house himself.

She was smiling to herself as they rode the elevator back to their penthouse, and Atom asked her what she was thinking. "Just, I get to see CEO Harcourt at work." Atom chuckled. "Which do you prefer? CEO or construction dude?"

"I prefer," and she pressed her body against his, "naked Harcourt to all other Harcourts."

"Minx." But he kissed her, his tongue exploring her mouth as his fingers tangled in her long hair. "Mrs.

Harcourt, when we get to our room…" The elevator dinged and stopped at their floor then, making them both laugh at the irony. "As I was saying… now that we're in our room, and all alone…"

He led her by the hand into the dark living room with the wall-to-ceiling windows but stopped her as she stepped towards the bedroom. "Uh-uh."

Maia smiled a little confused. "Baby?"

"I want you to stand in the middle of the room. Do you trust me?"

"With my life," she said softly, and he chuckled, pulling his necktie from around his neck and winding it around her eyes. "Kinky."

"Things are about to get really kinky, Miss Gahanna."

"Mrs. Harcourt," she shot back and laughed, "That's my name and I'm proud of it."

She felt him slip the straps of her dress from her shoulders, felt the silk shift slither down her body. Atom trailed a finger between her breasts then down her stomach, prodding her gently in the navel and making her giggle.

Then his hands slid around and unclasped her bra before sliding down to remove her panties. Maia shivered with pleasure as Atom stroked every inch of her skin… except he didn't touch her sex once, and eventually she protested and heard him laugh.

"So very impatient. Wait, my love, I promise it will be worth it."

Next moment she heard him pick something up, a sloshing of liquid then she shrieked as he sprayed cold liquid all over her, champagne she guessed. "Oh, you will pay for that, Harcourt." Then she cackled again as he swept her to the floor and began to lick every drop from her skin.

Soon she was a quivering mass of excitement as finally, finally, his mouth found her clit, and as he teased the small nub of electric nerves, Maia gasped for air, shuddering through orgasm after orgasm.

Being blindfolded was only adding to the excitement as Atom's lips roamed across her skin, his tongue replaced by his fingers on her clit now as he kissed her belly, running the tip of his tongue around the deep indentation of her navel.

"Oh God, Atom…" She wasn't crazy, it had never been this intense, and now she remembered where they had met, in that club, and wondered what he would have done with her there. "Atom… know this. I will do anything, try anything with you… anything."

He pushed the blindfold from her eyes and smiled down at her. "Baby… I want to fuck you against the window, your breasts and belly against the cold glass, have you look out over the city as I take you from behind, kissing your neck, your shoulders…"

Maia moaned and nodded, and he lifted her to his feet. "I want to strip you first," she said, and he nodded, smiling softly.

"I love you so much, Maia Harcourt."

She unbuttoned his shirt, pressing her lips to his hard chest. "You are my everything, baby."

He stepped out of his pants and Maia slid his underwear down his muscled legs. His cock was already hard as a rock, and when she took him in her mouth, Atom groaned with pleasure. Maia traced her tongue around the sensitive tip, up and down the long, thick shaft.

She drew at him, sucking and teasing as he tangled his fingers in her hair until he was coming, shooting creamy white cum onto her tongue. She swallowed him down as he drew her to her feet and kissed her with such passion it left her breathless and light-headed.

Atom pressed her against the cool of the window and Maia leaned her cheek against the cold glass, sighing happily as Atom trailed his tongue up her spine then kissed the back of her neck. He pushed her legs apart with his foot and eased into her, clamping his hands over hers, splayed on the glass.

He thrust harder and harder, and Maia lost her composure, moaning, crying out his name, completely under his control. They fucked with such an intensity then when they came, together, Atom turned around and they stared at each other for the longest moment.

"If there was a word stronger than love, I would say it to you, Maia… but there are no words for how I feel for you. I'll never want more than this, us… and maybe one day children of our own. For me, the day cannot come soon enough."

Maia kissed with a furious passion. "I've been yearning for a child with you. A child that will know her parents love each other and their children without condition, without restriction."

"You don't think it's too soon?"

She shook her head. "Our child will have something Luka didn't have… a father who would never, ever hurt her. A father she can trust to be her champion, her protector, her teacher." Unconsciously she had begun to use the female pronouns, she realized.

"And a mother who loves unconditionally. Who would walk into traffic for her." Atom stroked her hair behind her ear. "Luka did have that mother. And I am honored that you would bear my child with as much love as you had for her."

Maia kissed him again. "Take me to bed, Atom. All I want, right here, right now, is you. Always."

"Always," he agreed and carried back to tier bed, where they made love until a low winter sun broke over New York City.

Chapter Eighteen

"Well, girl, I have to say… you do look radiant, and thank God for it." Sakata smiled at her friend as they sat in the restaurant the next day. They were enjoying a leisurely lunch, chatting and catching up. "That man is doing you good."
Maia grinned. "He is, Sak, he really is, and it's not just Atom, but my whole life out there. It suits me, you know?"
"I can see that. A bookstore owner, a dog, a gorgeous man… all out in the beauty of Washington state. Makes me feel quite envious."
Maia chuckled. "You'd give up Fifth Avenue for that?"
Sakata reeled back in mock-horror. "Wash your mouth out, Gahanna." She laughed. "But we're very different, Maia, that's why I love you. I never said this but, before, with Zachary, in the world we live—"
"—I didn't fit? I know that now, don't worry."

Sakata's eyes were soft. "But I am forever thankful you were in it, Maia, never think that. It's just I always felt you were—" She cast around for the right word. "Caged."
"Funny, Atom said the same thing. I think you're right."
There was a small pause in conversation then Sakata chewed her lip. "Do you ever think about him?"
"Zach?"
Sakata nodded, and Maia shrugged. "Only to curse him, Sak. Every time I think of Luka, I hate him more. I think of how scared she must have been, how confused, and it makes me so angry—" Maia was aware her voice was rising, and she took a deep breath in. "Sorry. Listen, on that subject, before I saw you last night, I had a strange moment with the Molding-Ham."
Sakata snorted with laughter at the nickname. "She's been playing the grieving best friend for five years. It's getting a little old. She's a laughing stock."
"Did you see the article? Those Holy-Mother-Bless photos? Nauseous."
"And Photoshopped to Hell, yes. What was the strange moment?"
Maia told Sakata about the strange reaction Tracey had had to Maia asking her if she wanted to fuck a corpse.
"There was something in her eyes, like she was laughing at me for missing something so obvious."
"Like what?"
Maia hesitated then looked her friend directly in the eye. "Like Zach might be alive."
Sakata's eyebrows shot up. "That's crazy."

"Is it, though? After all this time, there's still no body, no actual evidence he's dead.. And something happened back in Washington."

"What?"

Maia told her about the hat they'd found in the attic of their house. "The more I think about it, the more I am certain that Luka was wearing it when she disappeared."

Sakata was silent then put her hand over Maia's. "Oh, darling."

The sympathy in her voice made Maia flush. "You think I'm crazy."

"Of course not. But, Maia, you have this new, incredible life. You're married to the love of your life. Darling, don't look back. Don't ponder on things you will never get the answers to. Zach's gone and so, sweetheart, is Luka. I'm so sorry, but for your own sake, don't look back."

Maia felt a sting, but she nodded. She knew Sakata was right, but she had almost wanted her friend to acknowledge there was something weird about the two situations.

Later, when she and Sakata had said goodbye—an emotional one in which they promised to stay in touch more regularly—Maia called Atom but got his voicemail. She decided to go Christmas shopping on her own, avoiding all the stores she used to go to with Luka or Zach—that wasn't her life anymore.

She told Ash, who was chauffeuring her everywhere on Atom's request, that she wanted some time alone, and though he wasn't happy about it, he'd been instructed to follow her orders by Atom. "Please though, take the panic button. Just in case."

Maia tried not to roll her eyes. "Fine." Anyone would think I'm the First Lady, she thought. She still wasn't comfortable with the protection Atom had set up, but this was the compromise. When she wanted to be alone alone, she was. She'd be fine in the stores with the amount of people around a few days before Christmas. Maia had to admit, she was so looking forward to her first holidays with Atom. This time last year, I was miserable and alone. Now I have the best husband, a home, real friends, and business I love. Her spirits lifted, and she spent the afternoon happily shopping for gifts.

Atom called her just before five p.m. "Where are you now?"

She told him.

"I'll come meet you. There's a great Korean place down the block from there. What do you think?"

"Yum. Now I'm starving! Hurry," she laughed as he chuckled and told her the name of the restaurant. "I'll meet you there."

"Ash around?" Maia almost laughed at the studied casual way he asked.

"Solo outing, Chewy."

Atom both sighed and laughed. "Fine. Pain in my ass."

Maia grinned. "Live with it. See you in a few."

Atom was waiting outside the restaurant when she found it, and he kissed her hello, not caring at the people staring at them. "Hello, beautiful."

"Good evening, handsome." She nuzzled her nose against his. "How was business?"
"Dull. Very dull." He grinned. "But let's go in. I'm famished, and I need food and you."
"In that order?"
"At the same time."
She wiggled her eyebrows at him. "Kinky."
He grinned and took her hand. In the restaurant, they sat at a small table in the window and chatted about their days. Atom ran a hand through his dark curls. "God, I'm glad we don't live here, baby. Too many people."
"I'll drink to that. I can't wait to go home, to be honest. I want our little house, our dog, our little piece of heaven."
Atom touched her cheek. "Hey, we can change the flights, you know. We could go tonight."
Maia smiled. "That sounds wonderful except…"
"Except?" He looked surprised given what she'd just said.
Maia giggled and leaned closer, lowering her voice. "Sakata told me about this club. An exclusive club." She held his gaze and realization dawned in his eyes.
"Really?"
"There's a special place inside the club. A room. A glass cubicle where people… you know. You can choose whether it's private or… it has this special glass. You just flick a switch, and if you want, everyone else can watch you fuck." Her face was burning, but she could see that her words were turning him on. "You can wear eye masks if you want, to hide your identity, but otherwise…" She put a hand to her burning face. "I just thought… with

you, God, it would be so freaking exciting. Have I shocked you?"

"Where did we meet? The second time?" Atom smiled but his eyes were intense. "Of course, you haven't shocked me… you've delighted me."

"So… yes?"

"Try to stop me, beautiful."

So engrossed in their planning and their love, they didn't see the man watching them from a table in the back. His eyes were riveted to Maia's face, watching as the new husband stroked it tenderly. How would he feel when she was gone? By the look in his eyes, he would be destroyed. Good.

Harcourt should never have touched what didn't belong to him. And Maia…

Fucking slut whore.

She would die slowly, he decided, and while she was dying, he would tell her the one thing that would make her death even more hopeless, even more pointless.

He smiled to himself. Not long now. Enjoy your lover while you can, Maia.

God, but she was so beautiful. Those gorgeous almond-shaped eyes with the thick dark lashes, the flush on her honey skin, that sweet smile. His groin tightened, and he remembered the feel of her skin, the flesh on her inner thigh, the way her vagina would pulse and tighten around his cock. It seemed impossible to him that he would never feel that again, but this was the path he had chosen.

He left money for his meal on the table and left, passing by Maia and her husband. He couldn't help but brush his fingers against her neck and had the satisfaction of feeling her stiffen as he walked away.

Outside it had started to snow. He reached in his pocket and pulled out his cell phone. He pressed the number for home and heard the ancient machine pick up. "It's me. I'll be home soon, and we'll eat supper together. Remember the rules. No lights on in the house until I get home. Remember. I don't want to have to punish you again. We both know what that would mean, don't we?"

He ended the call and headed for the subway, disappearing into the evening throng of people easily. That was his gift, after all.

Disappearing…

Chapter Nineteen

Maia's courage only started to fail as they walked into the club at almost midnight. Atom squeezed her hand. "You want to go, just say."
She shook her head. "I want to do this. I told you I wanted try everything with you, and God, I really, really want to do this."
He stopped before they reached the coat check and drew out two eye masks. "Yes?"
Maia nodded, somewhat relieved. Atom tied the white mask around her eyes and then she returned the favor. "Should we use false names?"
"You can be anyone you want to be."
"Just yours. Always yours."
"Then we don't need fake names."
He led her through the club. The interior was exposed brick, with alcoves where couples lounged on chaise lounges, some making love in pairs, or in threes or fours.

Beautiful waitstaff drifted around ethereally, barely clothed and silently serving drinks, not making eye contact.

The whole place had an otherworldly atmosphere about it—it could be a million miles away from the Manhattan streets above it. There was something Greco-Roman about the whole place—flowering plants dripped from the brick walls, low lighting, and sensual music.

Some couples, mixed and same-sex, were dancing, and for a few minutes, Atom slipped his arms around her waist, and they swayed to the music. Maia was grateful. It relaxed her and when Atom led her to the glass cubicle in the middle of the club, she followed him with a thrill of excitement running through her.

Inside, she was surprised at how clean and inviting the place was. The glass was switched to one way, so they had privacy—for now.

There was a bed, a small queen size with fresh sheets, and Atom swept her onto it. "Let's get relaxed first."

He unzipped her dress, and she stepped out of it. She'd bought new lingerie, a deep mauve bra and pantie set which looked good against her dusky skin and by the appreciation in Atom's eyes, he thought so, too. He ran a finger down the silky strap of her bra and smiled at her. "Beautiful, but they're going on the floor, because what's underneath is the real prize."

Maia felt absurdly flattered, and when he drew her panties down her legs, so gently, she felt even more beautiful when he looked up at her. Atom stood and freed her hair from the messy bun at the nape of her neck, letting it fall down her back. "You are the most beautiful creature on this earth," he whispered, his lips an inch from hers, "and I still can't believe you're mine."

"Always," she said and pressed her lips to his. Her fingers went to the buttons on his shirt slowly at first, but soon she was almost ripping it from him in her need to get him naked. She ran her tongue from his throat to his rippling abdominal muscles, feeling them quiver with pleasure. Atom chuckled and tumbled her to the bed, and they wrestled around playfully before he took her face in his hands and studied her. "I almost don't want to share you but keeping all this sexiness to myself is such a selfish thing to do."

"Only you get to touch me, my love. Only you."

Atom's hand slid between her legs and began to stroke. "Do you want to make love first?"

She shook her head. "Take me, Atom. Take me against the glass. Give everyone a master class in fucking."

Atom's eyes ignited with desire. "You dirty girl."

Maia giggled as he swept her up into his arms and carried her to the glass. For a moment they just looked out at the people outside. No one was looking at the cubicle and Maia was a little disappointed and said so.

Atom grinned. "You little exhibitionist. That's because they have no idea we're in here. When we decide—if we decide—to switch the glass to two-way, then the lights in the club go out, and they can see us."

Maia pressed her body against the glass and looked back at him over her shoulder. "Then let's give them a show."

Atom was on her then, kissing her neck, pressing her breasts, her belly against the glass. Maia moaned softly, then gasped as Atom's cock thrust hard into her sex. Her head rolled back, and he kissed her mouth as he fucked her. "Shall we?"

She nodded, and he flicked the switch to change the glass. For a scintilla, Maia was terrified as the lights changed, and she saw people in the club turn towards them. Then the adrenaline hit as Atom's pace quickened and Maia began to enjoy being watched. There was no judgement in their eyes, and indeed Maia saw admiration, desire, lust.

She came hard, gasping Atom's name and heard his groan of release as his cock pumped hot, thick semen deep into her belly. They caught their breath before disengaging and Atom flicked the glass back to one way. He turned her gently to face him, and she smiled at him tremulously. "That was such a rush."

He cradled her cheek in his palm. "You have made my fantasies come to life." He grinned. "Let's go home, baby."

Two hours later, they were on a private flight back to Seattle.

"You have dirty in your eyes," Lark said accusingly as Maia greeted her at the bookstore the next morning. "Please tell me you and Atom didn't just do it in the backroom again."

Maia grinned. "For the record, that was just the one time and no. We just had a great time in New York."

"Bah." Lark said, looking a little grumpy. "At least let me live vicariously through you."

"That's weird, Lark." But Maia laughed. Lark's record with boyfriends lately was showing signs of bad luck.

"Or I just have a broken picker," Lark said now. "Hey, by the way, you left your cell phone here. The pink one. I think I heard it buzz the other day which is how I found it. I don't know why you still have it, it's ancient."

Maia's smile faltered a little. "I know. It was the phone I had when Luka went missing. You'd think a five-year-old wouldn't remember a number by heart, but she did. I have it still... just in case."

Lark's expression softened. "Of course, sorry."

"No biggie. You heard it buzz?" Maia walked into the office and picked it up, noticing it needed charging. She plugged the lead into the electric outlet and saw the charging symbol appear, along with a missed call notification from an unknown number. "Probably spam," she said, not hiding her disappointment. "I can't believe I forgot to take it with me."

Lark put a hand on her shoulder. "Maybe it just means... you're healing."

Maia smiled at her young friend. "Maybe it does. I'm just not ready to give it up... yet." She chewed her lip. "Tomorrow is the five-year-anniversary. Maybe after Christmas."

Lark rubbed her shoulder again and left her alone. Maia stared at the phone, willing it to ring. "Oh, where are you, my darling Nugget? I would give anything to find you." She squeezed her eyes shut, willing back the tears. Don't do this. You have everything to go on for... for Atom. She smiled then. She loved him with all her heart, and she couldn't wait for them to have children.

She blinked and heard Lark's voice, raised and irritated. That was unlike her chilled out young friend. She heard Lark cry out and darted out to see her young clerk clutching her face and the retreating figure of a man running from the shop.

"He hit me! That God damned bastard hit me!"

"Are you okay?"

"I'm fine... Maia!"

But Maia was out of the shop, running after the man, incensed. She saw him turn into an alley behind a row of stores and followed him. She was raging now and as she got closer, she recognized him. It was the creep who had hit on her.

He turned a corner, and Maia followed him. Mistake. He was waiting for her. As she rounded the corner, he grabbed her, and too late, Maia realized she'd been set up for this.

Her attacker threw her to the ground and was on top of her, punching her hard in the stomach. Maia, winded, curled up into a ball, shielding her head as he rained punches down on her. Where the hell was Ash?

Maia wasn't a feminist for nothing though, and when her assailant paused, she sprang into action, sliding around on the icy ground and taking out his knees. He buckled, slipping and crashing to the ground. Maia scrambled to her feet.

"Maia!"

Finally, she heard Ash screaming her name. "Here… oh!" Her attacker's right fist connected with her temple and she dropped, dazed as he took off. Maia's head spun as Ash reached her, and he picked her up. "Are you okay?" She nodded, closing her eyes, trying to quell the dizziness. "He attacked Lark."

"I know, I'm so sorry. He knocked me out before… I never saw him coming."

Now she saw Ash's head was bleeding over his left eye. "God, Ash, we need to get you to a doctor."

But Ash insisted on taking her back to the shop first, then as Lark called the police and medics, Maia tended to Ash's bleeding head. "I think you need stitches."

"Maia, really, I'm okay. I'm more concerned about you." Maia shook her head. "Really, I'm good. I'll just be sporting a few nice bruises for the festive season." She sighed. "And I suppose I can't ask you not to tell Atom?"

"Already on his way, sorry. We have a panic button direct to him."

"Well, I suppose you're just doing your job."

Atom arrived just as the police did, and Maia had to hide a grin as he barked questions at all of them, stepping on the police officer's own questions. Eventually, the officer had to interrupt. "Sir, please. If we're to find this man…" Atom shut up then, but Maia could see the stress in his face, the worry. He kept glancing at her as if she would break down, but she took his hand, squeezing it. Eventually he couldn't stay silent anymore.

"The fact he came back for her, that he set this up, so she would be alone, unprotected…"

Ash flushed, and Maia felt sorry for him. Atom saw the other man flinch and put a hand on his shoulder. "I'm not blaming you, Ash. I just want a discussion on the motive… God, he isn't just some creep, is he? He wanted to hurt Maia. We're dealing with an obsessive."

He and Maia shared a long glance, and she could see he was wondering the same thing as he was.

"Did you recognize anything? Anything about him, ma'am?" The police officer had seen that look.

Maia shook her head. "I don't… I don't know."

"What does that mean?"

Maia felt desperate. "The only person who might want to hurt me… he is.. or was… he was much larger than this man. This man is skinny in the extreme, the eyes are the wrong color…" But as she said it, a certainty settled in her heart and she knew—or rather, she finally acknowledged it to herself. "But yes… it could be."

Atom's face was pale, and he closed his eyes. The officer looked between them. "Who?"

Maia looked at him. "My ex-husband. Zachary Konta," she said in a dead voice then turned and threw up.

Chapter Twenty

Maia watched as Atom checked every door and window in the house as she sat with Betty cuddled up on the couch. When Atom had finished his recognizance, he came down and sat next to her, his arm around her shoulders. "So."
"So."
They looked at each other. "He wants to kill me." Maia said it, but there was no fear in her voice, just resignation.
"He won't get near you." Atom's voice was crackling with anger. "Look, the police told me they were contacting New York. They're reopening the case."
"He killed her. He killed my daughter. Now he wants me dead."
"I don't get it… why now? Why not five years ago?"
"Because I was still his five years ago. Because I hadn't fallen in love with another man. I'll bet you any amount of money in the world that he's been watching me this

whole time, and he could hardly do that running across the country after me." She put her head in her hands. "It's over. Luka's dead."
She began to cry softly, and Atom wrapped his arms around her and let her cry herself out. Betty snuffled and licked the salty tears away. But it wasn't the hysteria she thought she would suffer when she finally said the words aloud. Just pure sorrow. "Luka…"
"I'm so sorry, baby."
They sat in silence for what seemed an age but then Atom looked up. "Unless he had help."
Maia wiped her face on her sleeve. "Help?"
"You said he couldn't follow you here unless he had help. What about that woman, the woman in New York?"
"The Molding Ham?"
"You said she reacted in a strange way when you said Zach was dead."
Maia stared at him. "She did." She thought about ti some more. "That fucking bitch. That fucking, fucking bitch!" Now she was angry, up and pacing. "I will fucking wring her skinny-ass neck!"
Atom calmed her. "I'm calling the police. They'll need to talk to her… Maia? Are you listening?"
Maia's eyes were wild. "You have to take me back there, Atom—tonight. We have to go back to New York…"
"… no."
She stopped. "What?"
"I said no." Atom took a deep breath and held her shoulders. "Sweetheart, we do this right. We do this right

so that if that woman knows anything, she'll have to tell it to the police."

Maia wasn't happy with that. "She won't tell them shit," she raged, jerking away from him. "The only thing that'll get her to talk is my hands around her neck."

"That's the thing that will guarantee her silence, Maia."

Maia knew she was right, but she was too angry to back down. "You promised me you would always, always be there for me, and what I need right now, more than anything is for you to let me do this my way."

"By getting arrested for murder? Because I guarantee you, they won't look generously on you if you end Tracey Golding's life. And if Luka is still out there somewhere…"

Maia walked out of the room and went upstairs before he could finish. She slammed into their bedroom and lay on the bed, trying to calm herself. She knew she was acting like a child, but she was too mad.

She was still awake when Atom came and laid down beside her, but by then, she had calmed down. "I'm sorry. I know you're right."

Atom stroked her face. "Darling, there is not one thing in this world that I want more than Luka back in your arms. But we have to do things right. Konta needs to be in jail, and so does Tracey, if she has been helping. But this is all conjecture at this point. Until we know your attacker was Konta for sure…"

"I know." She sighed. "I'm sorry I lost my temper."

He smiled at her. "No problem, honey. Kind of hot to see you all kick ass."

Maia chuckled softly. "What would I do without you, Atom?"
"You'll never have to find out, baby."

They made love and fell asleep. It was almost three a.m. when Maia woke, a strange noise from downstairs alerting her. She sat up, listening hard. Not an intruder, more like a…… cell phone. But it wasn't the ring tone of her day-to-day phone.
She scrambled out of bed and down the stairs, not caring if she woke Atom or Betty as she clambered to reach the small pink phone before the ringing stopped. She grabbed it, pressed 'Accept' and said hello, breathless and shaking, and when she heard the voice on the other end of the phone, her knees buckled and she dropped to the ground…
"Mommy!"

Chapter Twenty-One

Maia held Atom's hand so tightly it was beginning to go numb. As the helicopter flew over Washington state towards Portland, Atom tried to keep his wife calm but he knew it was impossible.
In the forty-eight hours since Maia had received that phone call she had been waiting for every day for the past five years, Maia had been wired and almost hysterical every moment.
Luka.
Luka was alive and somewhere on the west coast. That was all she could tell her mother between sobs, and when they had called the police, the FBI had gotten involved. They hauled in Tracey Golding-Hamm in New York who rolled almost immediately at the threat of prosecution.
It was all true. Zach Konta had taken Luka, and for five years lived off-the-grid, keeping tabs on Maia the whole time. When she had moved to Washington state, he had

moved Luka to Portland, so he could watch Maia in her new life.

Luka told the police that Zach told her Maia was dead, and it wasn't until a photograph of Maia and Atom together in New York was printed in a paper Zach accidently left behind that Luka knew the truth.

Zach had kept Luka locked up for five years in the basement of the houses he rented. He'd fed her well, given her books to learn from and a television set but otherwise, she hadn't seen daylight.

The police liaison told Maia and Atom not to expect too much. "Your daughter has spent some of her more formative years locked away from the world. She's a different little girl from the one you remember, but don't let that show. She's gone through so much."

Maia had cried long and hard, both from relief and joy, but also from rage that Zach had done this to her darling girl. Atom had calmed her, but now as they flew to the hospital in Portland where Luka was being treated, Maia felt both sick and afraid.

What if Luka rejected her? What if she couldn't be the best mother for her damaged daughter?

"Darling, stop beating yourself up. Just don't expect miracles. We have all the time in the world to rebuild Luka's life for her."

But Maia couldn't wait to hold her girl in her arms. She could hardly believe any of this was happening.

It was Christmas Day and snow covered the ground as they flew overhead. When Portland came into view and the helipad on the roof got closer, Maia felt her heart began to thump harder and harder. In a few moments they were being hurried through the hospital corridors. She's here… she's here… Maia felt breathless with anticipation.

"The doctor would like to speak to you before you see Luka," the liaison said, and Maia nodded, although every cell in her body was screaming to let them see her daughter right now…

The doctor smiled kindly at her. "I realize you must be anxious to see Luka, but I just wanted to prepare you. The last time you saw her, she was a five-year-old child. Now she's ten, a pre-teen, but her experiences are not that of normal children. She's older than her years and very guarded. She's very thin, a result, we think, from anxiety rather than from being denied food. She's very smart and can see through any kind of charade. So be honest with her. She prefers that. She doesn't like to be touched."

Maia choked back tears then. "Did he… did he hurt or…"

"No. From what we can surmise there was no physical abuse, but neither was there affection. What was her father like to her when you were together?"

"Very affectionate… or at least, he gave the impression of it." Maia gave a humorless laugh. "Everything was an act with Zach, it seemed. Doctor… please, I know you're telling me this for all our sakes, but I need to see my daughter."

"Of course." He shot a glance at Atom. "Mr. Harcourt…"

Atom nodded. "Just Maia for now. There's plenty of time for me to meet Luka. Let's not overwhelm her." He kissed Maia's temple, and she smiled at him gratefully, leaning into his embrace. "I love you," he whispered, and she mouthed it back at him.

She almost wished she could hold Atom's hand as the doctor led her towards Luka's room. The fear in her was only calmed by the knowledge that she was only a few steps away… five steps… three… two…
The doctor opened the door, and Maia stepped into the room, her eyes immediately going to the child sitting on the bed. The girl stared back at her. Luka was taller obviously, her limbs willowy, her dusky skin sallow, her eyes watchful and wary.
But to Maia, she had never seen a more beautiful sight. She found her voice eventually as she stepped, trembling, towards Luka. "Hello, Nugget… oh, Luka, Luka…"
She began to sob as she held her arms out to her daughter, and slowly, the girl uncurled herself and moved silently and gently into her mother's arms.
"Mommy? Is it really you?"
Maia half-laughed, half-cried. "It is, my darling… Oh, Luka… I'm so sorry, I've missed you so much."
Luka looked up at her, and Maia could see the conflict in her eyes. "Daddy told me you died." Her little voice cracked. "He said you'd been killed by a bad man and that we could never go home because the bad man would come and kill us, too."

Maia's arms tightened around her daughter. She could feel Luka's spine through her sweater, and she silently cursed Zach. "Luka… Daddy is a very sick man. In his brain, do you understand?"

Luka nodded, and Maia felt her little arms tentatively wrapped around her waist. "Mommy?"

"Yes, my love?"

"Who is that man? I saw a picture of you. I knew you weren't dead then, and that's why I stole Daddy's phone to call you."

Maia sat Luka back on the bed and knelt in front of her so Luka could see her face, know she was speaking the truth. "That's Atom, sweetheart. He's my husband. He's very much looking forward to meeting you. He wants to take care of you and me."

"Is he nice?" The wariness was back in Luka's eyes, and Maia stroked her little cheek.

"He is, darling. All he has in his heart is love. He already loves you."

"How?"

Maia smiled. "Because he loves me, and he knows that without you, I can't be happy. Plus," she tickled Luka's nose lightly, "because no one who knows you couldn't love you."

Luka looked away from her. "Mommy."

Maia felt a strange pang. *Zachary, you bastard.*

"Nugget…" She sighed. "Listen, what do you want? Anything, and I mean anything. What would make you feel better?"

Luka bit her lip. "I don't know, Mommy." She attempted a half-smile, her first, and Maia's heart burst with love for this girl. "Just Mommy. All I want is you."

Maia hugged her daughter to her. "Darling, I promise you, I will never ever let you be taken from me again, okay?"

They held each other for the longest time. "Mommy?"

"Yes, baby?"

"Where's Daddy?"

Maia stroked her daughter's silky hair, then buried her face in it, breathing in her scent. She smelled exactly like Maia remembered, a powdery softness. "We don't know, darling. The police are looking for him."

"What about that lady?"

"Which lady, Nugget?"

"The horrible blonde lady."

Maia tried not to grimace. "Tracey?"

Luka nodded. "Daddy and her... I heard them talking about getting rid of me."

Maia couldn't help the gasp of pure horror then, and tears began to flood down her cheeks. She made Luka look at her. "Listen to me. Daddy and Tracey will be in prison soon for what they did to you. No one will ever, ever hurt you again, do you hear me? Ever." She took a deep breath in. "Darling... I live on an island, a very pretty island with Atom, and we have a lovely house on a quiet street. We have a dog called Betty."

Luka's eyes lit up, and Maia smiled. "Do you want to see a photograph?"

Luka nodded, and Maia got her phone out and showed her a photograph of Betty. Then she showed her a short video of the dog playing, and Luka laughed as she saw Betty running to the camera and licking the lens.

That laugh made Maia's heart soar, and she wondered how long it had been since Luka was happy. "Darling, would you like to come home with us? We have a room for you, but because it's all been so quick, we haven't been able to decorate it for you. So, when you come, we can go pick up some stuff for it together, and you can choose anything you want."

Luka touched the photo of Betty. "Can she sleep on my bed with me?"

Maia smiled down at her. "Of course she can, I don't think anyone could even try to stop her. Betty is a fluffy ball of love, you'll see. She'll adore you right away, be your best friend."

There was a knock at the door and the doctor put his head in. "Everything okay?"

Maia nodded, but felt Luka move closer to her. *She's scared he'll take me away from her…*

"Doctor… how long do you think Luka will have to stay here?"

The doctor looked at Luka, hesitating but Maia nodded. "Anything we discuss should be in front of Luka from now on. She has final say in these decisions." She looked down at her daughter. "I told you, Nugget, you are in charge now. No one is going to stop from doing anything."

"Well," the doctor said, "I would prefer Luka to stay a couple more days, just to get her immunity up… we can arrange for you to stay with her, Mrs. Harcourt, that's no problem."

Maia looked at Luka who visibly relaxed and realized just how terrified her daughter was that she would leave her again. "That would be perfect, but if Luka wants to come home…"

"Then I don't see a problem. In a couple of days," the doctor said again, but with a smile. He looked at Luka, who nodded.

"Okay." She looked at Maia. "Can I meet Atom?"

Maia's heart pounded with love for her daughter. "Of course you can, he can't wait to meet you. Are you sure?"

Luka nodded, her eyes full of curiosity. "I'll ask Mr. Harcourt to step in," the doctor said, and Maia thanked him.

While they were waiting, Maia smoothed Luka's hair away from her chin. "You grew up, Nugget."

Luka's eyes were sad. "I wish… I wish it had never happened."

"Oh, sweetheart, so do I. I would do anything to go back to that day. I wouldn't let you out of my sight."

Another knock and Atom stepped slowly into the room. His smile was soft as he saw them. "Hey, you two."

Maia held her hand out to him, and he approached. Maia could see he was nervous. He crouched down Luka's height. "Hello, Luka, it's so good to meet you at last. Your mommy has been telling me all about you. She thinks about you every day."

Luka nodded, studying Atom, sizing him up. For a moment, there was silence, then Luka reached out and touched Atom's beard. "Soft," she said, curious. She hopped off the bed to get closer to him.

Maia held her breath, but then Luka reached her arms up. She wanted Atom to pick her up. Maia's heart, already wrecked, soared as Atom grinned and picked Luka up. "Hey kiddo," he said with a smile, and Maia's tears came again as Luka smiled at him. "Did your mommy tell you we have a room for you? It has two huge windows and a reading nook, and it's very near to the beach."

"We take Betty to the beach for her runs." Maia added, stroking Luka's hair. "You'll love it, darling."

Luka nodded and reached for Maia again. Atom handed her over, smiling at them both. "We'll celebrate a proper Christmas when we get home, my loves."

Later, when Luka had fallen asleep in Maia's arms, Atom excused himself and went to call his security team. "Make sure the house and perimeter are secure. We're bringing Maia's daughter home soon, and I don't want a hint of insecurity for them, understand?"

"Yes, sir. Of course."

After that, he went to find the FBI liaison. "Any news on the search for Konta?"

The agent shook his head. "Nothing. He's gone to ground. Luka told us she was alone in the house for three days before we found her. He abandoned her. Father of the Year, huh?"

Atom's anger was visible to everyone. "Give me five minutes in a room with that guy…"

"I hear ya. I have three of my own. The thought of just leaving them… man." The agent shook his head again in disgust. "This guy is scum."

Atom sat down next to him. "What worries me is he'll come after Maia. He's already attacked her twice. Now that she has Luka back and she's happy, he'll be psychotic in trying to get to her."

"We have the hospital covered, believe me. No one is going to touch her, either of them, here. There's a nationwide alert out for him with the new description you gave us, too. And the accomplice is singing like a bird, giving every bolt hole she knows of."

"Hmm." Atom wasn't convinced. "He's got unlimited funds and clearly the ability to disguise himself. What if he's never found?"

"We'll find him." The agent sounded confident, but then he looked at Atom and sighed. "Look, you can't live your life under threat. You have the means to secure yourselves, so do that, and man, enjoy having your family together."

Atom was touched that the agent considered them a family, and as he walked back to the room, he wondered again at how much his life had changed in such a short time, and how he'd gone from the single bachelor from a broken family to this happy little one. He wasn't a fool, he knew it would take time to build a relationship with Luka, to see how his and Maia's life would change now they had a child, but God, it excited him.

He went back to the room, saw Maia laying down now with Luka, and he climbed onto the bed next to his wife and put an arm around them both. Maia turned her head and smiled at him.

"I love you," she whispered. "Everything I could ever want is right here, right now."

Atom kissed her. "I feel the same way." He nodded at the sleeping child. "Does it feel strange to have her in your arms again?"

Maia shook her head. "It's just like I remembered except she's a little taller. She feels the same, she smells the same. My baby girl." Her eyes shone. "She likes you."

"And I like her. She's your image, Maia. Smart, too. There's no bull-you-know-what-ing her."

Maia stroked Luka's hair. "We are going to be the happiest family. I swear we are."

"I know," he said and kissed her again.

Two days later, they took Luka back to Bainbridge Island and began their new life as a family.

Chapter Twenty-Two

December turned to January, January to February, and soon spring was settling over the state and new growth began to flourish.

Luka thrived with Maia and Atom to help her. It wasn't easy—there were nights when she would wake up screaming, and Maia would run in to calm her hysterical daughter. Many nights she would have to sleep with her daughter to keep her from crying.

Through it all, Atom was the calming force for them, and he and Luka slowly got to know each other. Atom talked to her like an adult, respecting her experience and her pain, never overstepping, but soon Luka was learning to trust him as Maia did.

The day Luka went unbidden to hug Atom, Maia thought she might cry with happiness. She knew Atom was delighted and touched.

All three of them decorated Luka's room as she wanted, endless bookshelves, a permanent tablecloth fort at one end, a book nook at the other. As predicted, Luka and Betty fell in love immediately, and they went everywhere together.

Having missed five years of schooling, Maia hired a tutor for Luka to come to the house, but the tutor soon told them that Luka, if anything, was ahead of her peer group. Emory and Dante brought Nella to meet Luka, and the two girls, so alike in temperament and hobbies, bonded immediately. During the summer months, with Nella's help, Luka became more confident and outgoing, and by September, Luka was asking to attend the same school as Nella.

It had taken Maia a lot of courage to allow it, as well as Atom's and Emory's persuasion. "Maia, believe me, I'm all about school security given what happened to me." Emory had survived a school massacre and had saved the life of some students. "Which is why when we placed Nella, we made sure they had state-of-the-art security. Plus, Atom will have people outside the school at all times, I'm sure."

Maia still didn't seem sure. "It sounds like a prison."

"Just until they find Konta," Atom assured her, but they all knew that was looking more and more unlikely.

Almost a year after Luka was recovered, Zachary Konta had disappeared off the face of the earth. Tracey Golding-Hamm had been indicted on child abduction and other charges and was awaiting trial in New York City, much to Maia's satisfaction.

Sakata and Henry had visited for two weeks in the summer, and to Maia's delight, Luka had remembered them, especially Sakata, and didn't associate them with her father.

Luka never mentioned Zach. She'd talked to a therapist alone, at her own insistence. Maia asked her why she didn't want her to hear what she had to say, and Luka, showing maturity, had told her she didn't want Maia to hear the worst of it. "I know you have nightmares, too, Mommy."

Maia's heart ached for the childhood that had been taken from her daughter. She didn't show it in front of her, but when she and Atom were alone, she would cry for those years and the innocence that was lost.

Luka's eleventh birthday was a special day. Falling on October 13th, she had told Maia that she didn't want a party, just a day with her family. "Mom, can it just be you, me and Pa?"

Maia looked at her in shock, but Luka was looking at Atom, who looked as taken aback as Maia. Maia and Atom exchanged a look. "Sweetheart… Pa?"

Luka went to Atom, and she smiled shyly. "Pa." She said it simply, and Maia could see the emotion in Atom's face as he hugged her.

"Of course, it can, sweet thing." His voice sounded choked, and he cleared his throat, embarrassed but delighted. "Now, what can we get you for a present?"

Luka smiled and again Maia thought how old she looked.
"I only want one thing."
"Name it."
"I want a new name. I want to be Luka Harcourt, like Mommy. I've been practicing saying it, and it fits me now." She looked at Maia uncertainly, but Maia's eyes were full of tears and she smiled.
"It does."
Atom made Luka look at him. "Darling Lu, you know that more than anything, I wish you were my biological daughter, don't you? As far as I am concerned, you are my daughter. I love you so much, so, so much, and it's an honor you want my name. Of course… of course…"

Later, when Maia went to bed and found Atom in their bedroom, gazing out of the window, she went to him and found his cheeks wet with tears.
"Hey, hey, hey, what's this?"
Atom laughed, shaking his head. "I never thought this would be possible for me. This. A family. I thought I was too messed up, you know?"
Maia drew him into her arms. "You survived the worst that could happen to a child. You and Lulu have so much more in common than you think. I've seen the way you and she have become best friends over the past few months, and it's because you, out of both of us, lived that horror. The breakdown of parental trust. You get her in a way I never could, and I'm so fucking grateful, I can't tell you. Not that I would wish either childhood on you both,

but they did happen and now... you've helped her to heal, baby."

"She's helped me." Atom kissed Maia and cradled her face in his hands, his eyes intense on hers. "Loving you healed me in so many ways, Maia Gahanna."

"Harcourt," she said and laughed. "We'll all have the same name now."

"Can you believe she asked for it?"

Maia laughed. "I can. Actually, I can. She loves you, Atom... Pa."

"Wow. Pa."

Maia smiled and took his hand. "Come on, Pa. Let's go to bed and do Ma and Pa things. Maybe we'll make a little sibling for our girl."

They'd been trying to get pregnant for a few months—well, Maia had come off birth control, anyway—and now as they made love slowly, they knew that if and when it happened, their family would feel ever more complete.

Two months later, as Christmas approached, Maia was with Lark in the bookstore as Atom, Luka, Emory, and Nella shopped for gifts for Maia in the city. Maia waited until there was a lull in customers, then went back to the small bathroom in the backroom.

She snagged her purse and took it with her, digging into it to find the pregnancy test she had bought earlier.

She tried not to get her hopes up as she took the test and waited the few minutes to see the result, but something in her was changing, she knew that. She had felt it—a strange sensation that she might be pregnant—for the last week. Her period was late now, and this morning, she had ducked into the pharmacy before coming to the store.

She sat impatiently, willing herself not to look before it was time. She went out into the backroom, washing her hands in the sink, and then she grabbed the trash bag to take it out, hoping it would distract her long enough. She opened the back door and walked down the alley to the refuse bins, throwing the trash bag in.

Mai turned to go back into the store and froze. A man stood less than a foot from her. He had put on weight now, a lot of weight, and he'd bleached his hair, his eyebrows, his beard. His contact lenses now were an icy grey.

"Hello, Maia." Zachary said in a friendly tone as he drew the knife from his pocket. He moved too quickly for her as she tried to dart away.

She didn't even have time to scream.

Ash ducked into the store, rubbing his hands together. "I know, I know I'm not supposed to be in here," he grinned at Lark, "but I figured I could grab some of Maia's spiced apple juice to go. It's freezing out there. Where is she, anyway?"

"In the back. Maia?" Lark called, but when her boss didn't answer, she stuck her head around the door. "Huh. Guess she took the trash out. Don't worry, Kevin's watching the back."

Lark didn't seem phased, but Ash frowned and went into the backroom, sticking his head out of the door. There was no one outside, his colleague Kevin was nowhere to be found, but as he stared along the alleyway, he saw something on the ground. He went toward it, and as he approached, he cursed loudly. Blood.

"Jesus." He grabbed his phone as he walked back to the store, Lark looking worried.

"What is it?"

Ash's face was drawn and troubled. "It's blood. Maia's been taken."

Chapter Twenty-Three

Atom hit the brake and was out of the car before it had even fully stopped. Ash met him. "Boss… I can't even begin to—"

"Stop. Just tell me what's happened." Atom felt the panic in him rise when he saw the ambulance, and Ash told him that Kevin had been attacked by an unknown assailant. Atom stalked over to his injured security guard. "How? How did he get the jump on you?"

"Mr. Harcourt, he looks completely different to every photo, every description." Kevin's face was streaked with blood. "I was watching, but this is a public area, and we can't stop just anyone. He didn't approach the alleyway until he was ready to. He's bigger, a lot of extra weight and his hair…everything is bleached blonde."

Kevin looked so guilty, so defeated that Atom felt sorry for him. This was his, Atom's fault, and no one else's. After a year, Maia had insisted on lightening the protection, telling him that four people on guard all day at the store just was too much.

She's argued for one but compromised on two—Ash for the store front, Kevin to patrol the alleyway behind.

"I'd seen the guy for a few days. He was like clockwork. He got a paper from the vendor, then sat on the bench to read it. It never occurred to me he was watching for Maia to come out of the back because she so rarely does. It's usually Lark handling the trash when Maia brings in the signs at closing time. He was waiting. I'm sorry, boss, I dropped the ball."

The paramedic with Kevin shot Atom a look that said, 'Let me treat this guy.' Atom held his hand up. "Just one more minute, please. Kevin… he must have taken her away in a vehicle. Did you see anything?"

Kevin nodded. "Hyundai. White."

"Great," Ash said, "because that's not one of the most common cars on the road."

Atom shot his guard a look. "Does this street have security cameras?"

"Some."

"Get them. They can't have gotten off the island this quickly. She's here somewhere."

Ash, his face red from Atom's sharp tone nodded. "Sure thing, right away."

Atom had called the FBI the second Ash had called him, and they assured him they were on to it. He called the agent back now and related what Kevin had told him.

"We've already got agents on all the ferries," the agent told him, "and we're sending in a helicopter search team."

"We're trying to find some camera footage," Atom told him as he saw the local sheriff's car pull up. "And the local cops are here."

"We'll find her, Atom."

Atom had told Emory what had happened, and she had taken Luka back with her and Nella to their home. He called her now and relayed everything. "How's Lulu?"

"She's a smart kid, Atom. She knows something is wrong. I'm running out of things to tell her."

"Let me speak to her, Em, would you, please?"

Luka said hello in a voice that quivered with nerves.

"Hey, sweetie pie. Look, it's okay, just Mommy needs me right now. We both love you and please don't worry, okay?"

"Pa?"

"Yes, Nugget?"

There was a long pause. "Is it my Dad? Does he have Mommy?"

Don't lie. Maia wouldn't want you to lie. "Yes, darling, he does. But we're going to find them, and then he'll be in jail, sweetie."

"Is he going to hurt her?"

Oh God, please, no… "I promise you, I won't let him hurt Mommy."

He just prayed he wasn't telling her the worst lie of her young life.

Maia woke up in the trunk of Zach's car, pain wracking her body. Zach had stabbed her, and the force of the blow had knocked her to the ground where he bounced her head off the icy ground and everything went black. Now, she clutched her hand to the stab wound in her side and felt the damp sticky blood. It didn't seem too deep, but it bled continually, and she knew she was in trouble if she didn't stop the bleeding.

Where the hell was he taking her? Why hadn't he just killed her in the alley? And what had he done to Atom's security people? She had seen Ash outside this morning, but Kevin, the other guy had been nowhere to be seen in the alleyway.

Why didn't I check? I got complacent for one second… God, the pain in her side was getting worse. She felt the car slow and come to a full stop. Shit. Maia felt around in the trunk for anything to use as a weapon, but it was empty.

She blinked as Zach opened the trunk and she struggled as he yanked her out. "Stop fighting me, darling," he said, his voice not showing any strain as she tried to fight him off. "You know how this is going to end, Maia. You've always known."

They were somewhere on the coast, and now Maia recognized it as a part of the island that wasn't populated by many people.

A small boathouse stood next to the water and Zach dragged her into it, throwing her to ground. Pain tore through her as he bound her hands behind her back and turned her over.

He looked down at her. "So… we come to the end game. Here's what's going to happen now, Maia. I'm going to kill you slowly. Then I'll put your body into this boat right here, and I'll sail out to the middle of Puget Sound and kill myself. Whether they find our bodies before the elements or the ocean take care of us, we'll never know." He tore open her shirt, smirking at the wound already there. "This was nothing, Maia. A graze." He sat back on his haunches and sighed. "Have you anything to say to me?"

"Why?" She said, her voice steady. Maia knew no one could save her now, but she was damned if was going to die without knowing why he had done all of this. "Why did you do this, all of it? What did I do to you to deserve it?"

Zach smirked. "You were going to leave me."

That shocked her. "What the hell are you talking about?"

"You were fucking Harcourt even back then. I saw you together at the party. Out on the balcony. Obviously planning your next assignation."

Maia goggled at him. "Are you fucking insane? That was the first time I'd even heard of Atom, let alone knew who he was."

"I saw you, Maia." The knife was perilously close to her skin, and Maia took a deep breath. Keep him talking. Distract him. The rope around her hands was looser than Zach had realized, and she was working them free slowly. "There was no mistaking that… look between you. How long had it been going on?"

She sighed. "I never cheated on you, Zachary, and you can believe that or not." She tried to smile at him. "I loved you. I loved you until the moment you took my daughter away from me. Your daughter, Zach. What you did to her, I cannot forgive you for."

He slashed at her skin with the tip of the knife, and she cried out at the quick pain. "You forgive me?" His face was an inch from hers then, and his spittle flecked her skin. Maia didn't look away, seeing the rage, the madness in his eyes. "You fucking whore slut! How many of my friends did you fuck?"

"None of them, Zach. You imagined it all. But you know what? I wish I had fucked all of them, all of them, because then this would be something more than proof that you are fucking deluded. You're nothing but a sick, fucking asshole—" her words were cut off as Zach stabbed her, the breath knocked from her lungs.

As he wrenched the knife from her, he leaned and forced his lips against hers—and Maia bit down hard on his bottom lip, feeling the soft flesh give way. Zach roared and rocked back as Maia finally freed her hands. Ignoring the pain of her wounds, she rolled up and planted both feet firmly in Zach's chest, kicking with all of her strength.

Zach tumbled backwards, and she heard his head crack off a steel post. Praying the blow had killed him, she scrambled to her feet and kicked him in the groin as hard as she could before darting for the door.

Her hopes were dashed when Zach screamed with fury as she pushed the heavy door open and stumbled out. Maia heard the helicopter just as Zach, his head a bloody mess, started after her. She staggered over the rocks to the car Zach had abandoned and locked herself inside it. As she watched the helicopter close in, she flashed her headlights at it… S. O. S…

Zach tried to wrench the door of the car open, but Maia gave him the finger and started the car. Her wounds were bleeding copiously now, and her head was dizzy. Don't pass out now. She yanked the car into reverse and screeched backwards, Zach still hanging on the door handle. She was dragging him and now she didn't care. "Die, asshole…"

She was distracted and didn't notice the stone boulder behind the car until she hit it with a shock. The force of the sudden stop made her hit the steering wheel, and she gasped as it struck her hard in the chest. The driver's window shattered as Zach threw a rock at it, and then he was dragging her out onto the asphalt.

Maia was losing the strength to go on, but Luka's face floated across her mind. As Zach, having lost his knife, fixed his hands around her throat and began to squeeze, Maia thanked God that Luka would have Atom in her life, to raise her, to give her all the love in the world…
Black spots danced at the corners of her eyes as she heard shouts, then gunfire, and as she passed out, she felt a weight drop onto her and something warm and liquid pumping onto her. Blood.

But not hers.

"Maia!"

Light seeped into her brain, and she opened her eyes as Atom hauled Zach's body from her and scooped her into his arms. "Oh my God, Maia, Maia…"

She focused on his beautiful face—and smiled. "It's over," she said. "It's finally over. I love you so much, but I think I have to pass out now, okay?"

Atom was laughing and crying at the same time. "You do what you need to, my love. We're going to get you to the hospital, okay?"

"Okay." She leaned her head against his hard chest and let herself sink into unconsciousness.

Chapter Twenty-Four

She felt little fingers curling around her hair as she woke, and she was smiling before she even opened her eyes. "Hey, my little Nugget."
Maia opened her eyes and smiled down at her daughter. Luka was cuddled next to her on the hospital bed, her head on Maia's shoulder. Atom was on Maia's other side, holding her hand. He bent down and kissed her. "How are you feeling?"
"Actually good," she said with a little surprise.
"That'll be the morphine." Atom grinned, nodding to the drip.
"Nah, it's the company," Maia said with a laugh. She kissed Luka's forehead. "You okay, Nugget?"
Luka nodded but didn't say anything, and Maia shot a glance at Atom, who gave her a smile and mouthed "She's okay."

Maia stroked her daughter's hair. "Sweetie, I really am okay. Your father… he's gone now. He can't hurt any of us anymore, but it's okay to feel sad."

"I don't feel sad," Luka said in a small voice, and Maia realized that her daughter was feeling guilty for not mourning her biological father. She hugged her close. "That's okay, too, Nugget, you know? Daddy was a very sick man, and he hurt us all. It's okay to be relieved." She kissed her daughter's forehead. "Okay, now?"

Luka nodded.

Later, Emory came to pick Luka up and take her home for a sleepover with Nella. At first, Luka was hesitant to go, but Maia persuaded her. "I'll be right here tomorrow, sweetheart, and home soon, I hope. I love you."

When they were alone, Atom took Luka's place on the bed, cradling his wife in his arms. "You scared the hell out of me."

"I took things for granted and let my guard down, and he got through. Don't blame Ash or Kevin, please."

"Ash quit. He's pretty cut up about letting you down."

"Ah, damn it."

Atom shrugged, and Maia saw residual anger in his eyes. "Atom, it really wasn't his fault. Zach was going to get to me one way or another. It's over now. He's gone, thank God."

They held each other for the longest time without speaking. Atom kissed her temple. "Is there something else you want to tell me, baby?"

Maia frowned. "What?"

Atom got up and grabbed his coat, pulling a brown paper bag out of it. "Lark found this in the bathroom the day you were taken."

Maia reached in and felt the plastic of the pregnancy test. Her mouth rounded into an 'Oh.' "I completely forgot about this. I took it, then tried not to look at it, tried to distract myself, so that's why I went to take the trash out." She felt a pang as she looked at him. "Did you look?"

Atom nodded, but she couldn't read his expression. "Take a look."

For a moment, she panicked. Her wounds, although nasty, hadn't been too serious—she'd been in surgery less than an hour—but if...

"Maia, take a look."

She pulled the test from the bag and made herself look at it. There were no double blue lines, but this wasn't one of those tests. This was a Pregnant/Not Pregnant test.

And it was clear. Pregnant.

Maia's hand flew to her mouth. "Oh my God…" She looked up at Atom whose smile was tremendous and delighted. "We're going to have a baby?"

Atom chuckled. "So it seems… the doctor confirmed it while you were in surgery, and everything is fine." He sat down again and kissed her. "About six weeks, they think."

"We're going to have a baby!" Maia was crying now, smiling through her tears as Atom took her into his arms and kissed her tenderly.

"Luka's going to have a brother or sister. We have a family, baby."

Maia held onto her husband, the love of her life, and cried with joy as he kissed her. "Thank you, Atom. Thank you for bringing me back to life in so many, many ways."

"Thank you for teaching me to trust again," he said, his voice gravelly with emotion. "From now on, we'll always, always be together, all four of us." He grinned. "Sorry, forgive me—and Betty, too."

Maia stared at him, joy flooding her system, taking away any last vestiges of pain or fear. "We're going to be so happy from now, aren't we, Atom?"

His green eyes twinkled at her. "There's nothing in this world more certain than that, darling. Nothing, I promise you."

And finally, after everything that had happened, Maia knew that to be true…

The End

While You Were Gone Extended Epilogue

Eight years after Maia Gahanna and Atom Harcourt marry, they are about to see their daughter Luka graduate from high school and go off on a gap year, travelling Europe. Both are overjoyed but know they will soon feel 'empty nest' syndrome, Maia especially, as she missed five years of Luka's childhood when her ex-husband kidnapped Luka.

With their young son, Eddie, enjoying a vacation to Disneyland with the Harcourt's best friends, Emory and Dante Harper, Maia and Atom can enjoy some quality time to themselves and decide to revisit a sex club in New York where they once spent an erotic night, and learn whether the passage of time has dulled their adventurous side, or if they're still open to new and sensual experiences.

When they meet the beautiful, androgynous Dae-Kim at the club, they have to make the choice whether they will include someone new in their lovemaking… just for the experience…

… just for the rush…

Luka Harcourt caught her father's eye and they grinned at each other. Luka then turned to her mother, rolling her eyes. "Mom… you promised you wouldn't cry."
Maia blinked rapidly to get rid of the tears. "I'm not crying, it's just allergies."
Atom snorted and hugged his wife. "Sure it is, honey."
"Momma, you're crying because Lulu is going away, isn't that right?" Eddie, their six-year-old had yet to learn subtlety and Maia grinned.
"Busted."
They were sitting around the kitchen table eating breakfast. Later, Luka would be graduating from high school, joint top of the class with her best friend Nella. Nella was the daughter of Maia and Atom's best friends, Emory and Dante Harper, and the two girls had been inseparable since the day they had met seven years ago.
Maia looked at her daughter now. Luka was eighteen and she could barely believe it. Tall, athletic and gorgeous, Luka was sweet but also funny as hell and a more rounded person than she had any right to be given her troubled upbringing.
Luka's biological father, Zachary Konta, had abducted her when she was five and for five long years, Maia had thought her beloved girl was dead. It was only after Zachary had gone completely insane and tried to kill Maia that the truth came out.

Maia reached out and ran a hand down Luka's long silky hair. "Everything packed and ready?"

After the ceremony, after a celebration meal, they were driving Luka and Nella to SeaTac airport to catch their flight to Paris. The girls were heading out for a year of travelling around Europe and although Maia was delighted for her daughter, she couldn't help but feel the clutch of fear in her belly for her daughter.

But Atom had been her counsellor when she expressed her doubts to him privately, in their bedroom at night where Luka couldn't hear them. Atom had listened to Maia's concerns but then taken her face in his hands. "Remember when I told you I'd never put you in a cage? That goes for Luka too."

"I know, I really do know that." She took a deep breath and Atom kissed her.

"Listen, it's not like she's going to be slumming it. They have all the hotels booked, all checked out by yours truly. We know their itinerary. Luka knew before they finalized everything the strain her being away would put on you. She feels it too, which is why she allowed Dante and I to fund safe places for her and Nella rather than doing the nomad thing. Luka was thinking of you."

"Which makes me feel so bad but I guess I can't have it both ways."

"Nope." Atom kissed her again. "And look, most of the places she's going, we have people there. Friends. Ivo in Paris, Maceo in Venice for starters."

Maia sighed and laid back on the bed. "You're right."

Atom looped his arm around her shoulders and pulled her close. "It's perfectly understandable you feel like this. You thought she was gone for so long. Everyone understands."

He began to make love to her then and Maia feel better, but now, sitting at the table for the last time as a family for goodness knows how long, she could feel the nerves reappear.

Thankfully, as soon as Nella arrived so the girls could get ready together for the graduation ceremony, Maia had Emory to sympathize with her. The two men, Atom and Dante, made fun of the teary women, making little Eddie laugh.
"You, you little monster," Emory picked up her godson and cuddled him, "I get to keep you for a whole weekend. How do you like that?"
Eddie grinned at her, adoring his 'aunt', wrapping his little arms around her neck. The Harper's were taking Eddie to Disneyland with them and their presumptive adoptive new son, Olly. They were in the final process of adopting the young boy and this was going to be a test of whether Olly would finally choose them. Emory wasn't worried—she and Olly had fallen for each other when they first met and she wanted him to have a friend his own age when he finally came to live with them.
Maia was wondering now whether she could cope being away from both of her children, but she wouldn't go back on her word now. Eddie was beside himself with excitement at the thought of going to Disneyland and he was so laid back and friendly, that Maia knew he would help Olly settle in.
And besides, Maia thought, as she went upstairs to check on the girls, she and Atom too would be having their own adventure. They were going to spend the weekend in Manhattan, seeing their old friends Sakata and Henry for dinner tomorrow evening and then, the following evening, Atom had dared her to return to the sex club

where they had spent an incredibly erotic evening, fucking in front of strangers, completely uninhibited.

Of course, that had been eight years and another baby ago… not that Maia was worried about her body. She'd never been the scrawny nor athletic type, however much she worked out, her curves remained and even now, in her mid-thirties, she knew Atom loved every inch of her and he was the only one she cared about.

But she hoped she would still have the bravery to go through with whatever they tried in the club. They wanted to be fearless, try something new and exotic—she just didn't know what and it kind of freaked her out.

"Mom?"

Maia blinked back into the present as Luka twirled for her. The lavender dress she wore made her honey-colored skin glow and the beads on the bodice caught the light and reflected in her eyes. Maia's eyes filled with tears again. "Oh, Lulu…" Her voice caught and broke.

Luka rolled her eyes and nodded towards Nella, who stood shyly in her own dress, a dark gold lace which fell to her mid-thigh. She had inherited Emory's staggering beauty, her dark caramel skin and big brown eyes. She giggled as Luka made a fuss over her and hugged her. "My beautiful girl," Luka said and the girls exchanged a long look that made Maia's heart warm. They may not have spoken it aloud to anyone, but Maia had guessed their secret a while ago and couldn't be more delighted.

"Babe? Kids? Car's waiting."

Then it was a frenzy of grabbing everything they needed and driving to the high school. It all went by in a flash. As joint-valedictorians, Nella and Luka gave a speech, finishing each other's sentences, making everyone laugh with their infectious humor and getting a standing ovation afterwards. Maia and Emory were openly weeping now, and even Dante and Atom looked red-eyed.

At the party afterward, Luka and Nella managed to split their tie between their friends and their families and by the time they had changed into their traveling clothes and were in the car on the way to SeaTac, Maia couldn't believe the day had flown by so quickly.

No-one was holding back the tears as they said goodbye to the girls and it took a while for them to even begin to walk through to the departures lounge. Atom hugged Maia to him. "Don't cry, baby."

Dante was holding Emory's hand. "Hey, look, as long as they don't come back pregnant or married to strange men…" He was trying to make a joke but his voice quivered.

"Right?" Atom nodded.

Emory and Maia shared a look and burst out laughing. Dante and Atom looked at them then each other. "Did we miss something?"

"Quite a lot, apparently," Emory said, chuckling and wiping her eyes. The men still didn't get it and Maia grinned.

"They might come back married, boys, but there won't be anyone else involved."

Emory leaned over to Maia. "Let's see how long it takes to get this… three… two…"

"Oh." Atom's eyebrows shot up and he looked in the direction of the retreating girls. They could still see them in the distance, and now it was obvious that they were holding hands. "Oh."

Emory and Maia chuckled as a smile spread across Atom's face. "Really?" He asked his wife who nodded. "Really?"

"That's fantastic."

Maia felt a warm feeling go through her at her husband's easy acceptance—not that she ever doubted it.

Dante still hadn't clicked. "What?" He said, his eyes huge. "What? What did I miss?"

Emory grinned and wrapped her arm around her husband's waist. "Come on, you. I'll tell you in the car."

Later, after everyone was in the know, Emory and Dante took Eddie back to their home with them, Maia kissing her son goodbye with more tears but not nearly as much trepidation. She trusted Emory and Dante with her child's life.

At home, their dog Betty. Now an old girl with arthritic hips but still the same love for her family, greeted them and they carried her up the stairs to their bedroom. Atom set her on the bed, but after Betty had kissed them both hello with her gentle licks, she got down from the bed and went out to the hallway. They kept her basket there for 'alone times'—which weirdly Betty always knew were off limits for her.

"It's either sweet that she knows we're in the mood, or she's a furry little pimp," Atom said with a grin and Maia laughed.

"She's a woofy genius, our girl." She went into the hallway and bent to kiss the dog's silky head. Betty licked her face again then got up and went into Luka's room, hopping up onto the bed and curling up on the pillow. Maia's heart hurt again. "I know, sweetie. I already miss her too."

Maia went back into their bedroom, stopping at the door as she watched him undress, unbuttoning his shirt, then stepping out of his pants. When he stood in his underwear, he looked up and smiled at her scrutiny. "Like what you see?"

"Always." She went to him, running her hand over the firm plains of his chest, his stomach, then moving down to cup his cock through his underwear. It felt hot and heavy in her hand and it quivered as she stroked it through the cotton. She stood on her tiptoes to kiss him. "Put that inside me," she whispered, "and fuck me into tomorrow."

Atom's eyes were intense on hers, his face dead serious for a moment, then his smile cracked wide across his mouth and he tumbled her onto the bed. "You want this, baby?"

"God, yes," she said, giggling, trying to keep up the seductress pose but failing, laughing like a giggly teenager until with one, firm, hard thrust he was inside her. His cock plunged deep into her sex, her clit on fire from the pressure of his fingers and Maia shivered and moaned until her orgasm took her over and she arched her back up as Atom slammed his hips against hers.

Afterward, she lay in his arms. "It just keeps getting better and better," she said, not a little smugly and Atom laughed.

"See, when you get the chemistry right…"

"Agreed, hubby." She stroked a hand down his chest. "Of course, I'm not that experienced, but I can't imagine it getting any better."

Atom chuckled and kissed her forehead. "There was no-one before Zach?"

"No." Maia's smile faded a little at the thought of her psychotic ex-husband—now thankfully long dead and buried. She blinked and smiled at Atom. "Don't you ever miss the clubs, the multitude of women just waiting for a taste of the Harcourt lovin'?"

Atom laughed. "Hell, no. I knew the second I met you

that I would willingly give it all up for one night with you, so now that we have a lifetime together…"
She kissed him. "Damn, right." She rolled onto her stomach, on top of him and stroked his face. They stared at each other for the longest time.
"You is beautiful," he said and she grinned, immediately crossing her eyes and blowing out her cheeks. "Even like that."
Maia grinned. "I wonder what we'll pluck up the courage to do at that club?"
"There's a world of options. If all else fails, we still have the glass cubicle."
"Yeah, but I want to try something new too."
Atom stroked her hair back from her face. "Like? We could try the pain rooms?"
Maia considered. "We do spanking and stuff here."
"They have crops and whips…"
"Is that what turns you on?"
Atom shrugged. "Not really. Okay, well, we'll just see what takes our fancy when we get there. We can just be whatever."
"We can." Maia pressed her lips against his. "We can just be. Now," she slid her hand down to his cock, felt it twitch and respond to her, "let's just practice some more, right now."
Atom grinned and rolled her onto her back. "Whatever you say, my darling one."

The next night in Manhattan, they were greeted by their friends Henry and Sakata. Sakata, a beautiful Asian-American woman with jet black hair and a wide cheeky smile, hugged Maia hard. "How're you taking the empty nest?"

"It's hell," Maia grinned at her friend. "But Lulu's already called me from Paris twice. She's so excited."

"Good for her... and have you finally clued Atom in on her and Nella?" Sakata already knew the answer to that, Maia having called her to set Atom up for a joke.

"Ha ha." Atom said, knowing he was being ribbed. "I think it's wonderful."

Over dinner, they talked about everything under the sun. Sakata and Henry were celebrating twenty years together now. They were childless by choice but adored their 'niece' and 'nephew' and often flew to Washington state to visit with them.

Sakata and Henry looked happier than they had in years and later, alone in the ladies restroom, Maia prompted her friend. Sakata grinned. "We are having, shall we say, a little renaissance? We've been seeing another couple."

Maia's eyebrows shot up. "Seeing?"

Sakata gave a filthy giggle. "Sleeping with, swinging, the old keys in the fish bow thing. Things had been getting stale and so we talked about it and honestly, boo, the sex has never been better."

Maia gaped at her and was speechless for a moment. Sakata grinned at her. "Come on, Maia, don't tell me you and Atom haven't ever gotten a little freaky?"

"Well, yes, but that was... um, we didn't sleep with anyone else."

"Details."

Maia flushed but told Sakata about the glass cubicle at the club. Sakata was impressed. "But I don't think I could cope with seeing Atom having sex with another woman. Not that I'm the jealous type but... god, I don't know."

"It's not always about sex. Both I and Henry have never had penetrative sex with the other couple, it's more about the fun, the touching, the arousal of it. Look." She got out her phone and Maia looked alarmed and Sakata laughed. "Don't worry, no nudes, I just want to show you how gorgeous they are."

She gave her phone to Maia and she saw a very attractive couple smiling at the camera. "They are very striking."

Sakata gave a giggle. "You're still shocked."

"A little I have to say, but I'm not judging. If it works for you…" Maia looked over at Atom. "I just can't imagine ever being attracted to anyone else."

"You never know. Someone might come along who surprises you."

Later, in bed back at their hotel, Maia told Atom what Sakata had told her and Atom nodded. "It had crossed my mind to suggest it, but it's tricky."

"How so?"

"I wouldn't want you to think that I wanted anyone else, because I do not." He chuckled. "I was a pussy, I was waiting for you to say it."

Maia laughed and pretended to beat him. "So very passive aggressive."

Atom laughed, wrestling her onto her back. "Think about it. We men get a bad reputation for not keeping our dicks in our pants. If you, wifey, suggested it… we're let off the hook because everyone assumes we're all programmed to want to see two women together."

"So, you'd want to do it with another woman?" Maia felt a little disappointed but Atom grinned at her.

"Either. Male or female, it would entirely be up to you."

Maia had to admit talking about her was getting her a little hot and Atom's open-mindedness only made her more aroused. "You'd consider a guy?"

"For you, always."

Maia pressed her lips to his. "Just so you know, I'll never

want anybody but you."

"I know that, baby. I have complete trust in you, don't ever question that."

"And I, you."

Atom kissed her softly. "You are my world, Maia Harcourt. Now," he said, with a wicked grin, "open those long, sexy legs of your and let me in."

Maia giggled and wrapped her legs around his waist as he slid his huge, thick cock into her. She sighed happily as they began to make love and smiled up at him. "I love you, baby. So, so much."

"Quiet, woman, I'm giving you my best moves," Atom grinned, making her bust out laughing and for the rest of the night, the made love and played games until both were exhausted and sated.

Maia was strangely nervous as they walked into the club again. It had been a long time but the club still had the chilled out, laid back atmosphere she remembered. For some reason, she expected to see clientele she recognized, which was weird because she didn't remember anyone, just Atom, from that wonderful erotic night.

The biggest difference was that they had decided to leave the eye masks at home. "Let's be brave," Atom said. "Besides, if we're really going to be doing this, I want to see their face."

Maia had been on the point of calling off the threesome all day, trepidation clutching her heart, but now she was here, she felt more relaxed. She and Atom found an alcove, a padded red velvet chaise lounge to sit on, and Atom ordered them drinks from the gorgeous waiter who came to serve them. "And two shots of Absinthe."

Maia goggled at him. "Really?"

Atom grinned. "All in?"

"All in."

The drinks helped steady her nerves and an hour later, they were so relaxed, they almost forgot why they were there. Atom was kissing her neck and Maia was stroking his groin through his pants, feeling how hard he was for her. Atom slid one shoulder strap down her arm, and exposed her breast, and Maia wasn't fazed at all. His attention and the alcohol were making her feel beautiful and sensual, and she saw some of the other patrons looking at her with open desire.

She turned her eyes to her husband. "I'm yours, forever, baby."

"I'm the luckiest man in the world," he murmured, his lips against hers.

Both were getting aroused that they would have begun to fuck right there and then, but something stopped them, a change in the atmosphere of the club.

A hushed awe. Both Atom and Maia saw the newcomer at the same time as the rest of the club turned their eyes to the ethereal being drifted through their midst.

He was the most beautiful man Maia had ever seen, and by beautiful, she meant beautiful and not handsome. His delicate features were perfect, his high cheekbones and pouty mouth highlighted with blush and gloss, his almond eyes soft but confident and lighter than his Asian features would normally dictate. Maia guessed contact lenses. He was tall, wearing a light grey suit, his hair dyed silver and cut short. Two diamond earrings in his ears complete the androgynous look. He seemed aware of the crowd's scrutiny and a small smile played around his mouth.

"Wow."

Maia looked at Atom who was staring at the newcomer.

He looked back at his wife and a silent communication passed between them and Maia nodded. She wasn't even sure if the newcomer was human, he was so ethereal in the way he looked and moved that she could easily imagine he was an angel.
Or a demon. There was also something mischievous about him. He leaned back against the bar, studying the clientele until his eyes fixed on Maia's and he smiled. Maia watched him stop a waiter and ask him something, then a second later, the waiter came over.
"Mr. Kim would like to buy you both a drink… in the private Shadow Suite."
The Shadow Suite was the most exclusive suite in the club, a sensually lit bedroom with a huge four-poster bed and a myriad of toys for the discerning clientele.
Maia and Atom looked at each, both nodding at the same time. Atom got up and offered her his hand. They followed the waiter, the angelic man already having disappeared, so confident of their agreement.
Atom leaned down and put his lips to her ears. "You want to stop at any time, just say so, but listen… anything that happens in there stays in there, okay? Anything goes, baby."
Maia smiled up at him. "Are you sure about this? I mean, I'm worried you'll leave me for him—he's way prettier than me."
Atom laughed, completely comfortable in his masculinity. "Not possible."

Atom opened the door to the Shadow Suite and the angel nodded at them. "Hello."
"Hello." Maia flushed, shyly. God, it was like looking at the sun. For a moment, she felt inadequate but then the angel smiled and it was such a cute, friendly smile that all

her fears fled.

"Dae-Kim. Or just Dae." the angel said and held out his hand to them. Atom shook it.

"I'm Atom. This is Maia."

"Hey Atom, Maia. Beautiful names." Dae smiled at Maia and kissed her hand. "May I pour you some champagne?"

"Please."

Dae handed them each a flute and gestured to the couches. "Why don't we talk?"

They sat and Maia wondered what the protocol for this kind of thing was. Dae saw the doubt in her eyes. "Don't worry, Maia, if all that happens tonight is that I enjoy drinks and talking with new friends, I shall quite happy."

His skin was so smooth she couldn't believe it. Not a hint of a five o'clock shadow. His features were delicate, the work of an artist, but his eyes... close-up now she could see they were definitely contacts, the unnatural grey of them a giveaway, but they suited his otherworldly aesthetic.

Atom asked Dae about his life—he was an entertainment lawyer based in Seoul who also had offices in Manhattan. He was in his mid-twenties, a lover of music, dogs and minimalism. "And bisexual... or rather, pansexual." He smiled at them both. "I have my favourite clubs in the major cities around the world. I'm never in one place long enough to form long-term relationships, but neither am I immune to loneliness. I think we all need the human touch from time to time."

Atom nodded, but Maia, who was fascinated by Dae, had to ask. "You are human, right?"

Both men busted out laughing and Dae nodded, patting Maia's hand. "I am, darling Maia. Very human. All this—" he indicated his face, "—is my safety net. A mask. It gives me the confidence to do this. Otherwise I'm just a kid from Busan."

Maia warmed to him, to his honesty. If he'd kept the aloof, ethereal thing up, she didn't know if she could have gone through with this but he was so… down to earth. She smiled at the juxtaposition of this angel being so earthbound.

Atom stroked Maia's hair, as if sensing she was relaxing. "Look, we'll be honest too. The first time we even discussed this was last night, and to be honest, if you hadn't walked in, we might have abandoned the idea." He chuckled. "I'm heterosexual but I can appreciate a beautiful man."

"Thank you," Dae said with a shy incline of his head, "the same to you."

Atom raised his glass. "To new friends."

"New friends."

Maia saw the question in Dae's eyes, saw the slight incline of Atom's head as if he were giving his blessing. Dae smiled, putting his glass down and coming to sit by Maia. He placed his hand on her face, cradling it gently and slowly pressed his lips against hers. They were so soft, his kiss sweet and inquiring. Atom swept the hair away from the back of her neck and kissed her there, his fingers at the zipper on her dress, pulling it down.

"Tonight is all about you, Maia…"

Dae nodded, holding her gaze. "Yes, it is."

It was heady, these two drop-dead-gorgeous men attending to her, and a little nerve=wracking. She had to decide right then whether she could let herself go.

"Wait," she said softy and both men paused.

"Dae… one thing. I want to do this, but I can't… go all the way with you."

Dae smiled and stroked her face. "Understood, sweet one."

"Is that okay?" Maia looked nervously between them, and she saw the love in Atom's eyes… and the relief.

"Of course… there's so much more to love making that we can enjoy."

"Atom's right, Maia. Just let us hold you."

And so, she did. Atom drew her dress down and she stood to let it slither to the floor, shivering with pleasure as Atom ran his hands down her sides. She leaned back on him, feeling his lips on her shoulders as Dae kissed her belly, running his hand up her thigh. She saw him cast another questioning look at Atom and felt warmed that he respected her husband enough to ask the question.

"Let's lay her on the bed, Dae." Atom picked her up and carried her to the bed. He stroked her face and kissed her. "Tell us what you want."

"I want to see you undress each other," she said, shocking herself as she said it but neither Atom nor Dae seemed phased.

It was incredibly erotic watching her husband undress this beautiful man. Dae's body, in clothes, looked like it would be fragile, reed-thin, but naked, he was toned, his abs muscled and taut. Standing together, he and Atom made a spectacular pairing and it made Maia's sex flood with arousal.

"Kiss him," she whispered and Atom smiled. Dae pressed his lips against her husband, a brief but sweet embrace.

When they broke apart, Atom looked at Maia. "Enjoy?"

She nodded, but then beckoned them over. "I'm getting lonely over here." She was feeling braver by the moment, and when they laid down with her, Atom behind her, spooning her, Dae stretching his long body next to her, Maia feltlike she was in a dream world.

When they began to caress her, she wanted to cry because the sensations they evoked in her were like a wildfire in her veins. Atom slipped his hand between her legs, stroking her, feeling how wet she was, while Dae kissed her lips, her throat, her breasts.

For the next hour, they stroked, kissed, and drove her towards an incredible and when finally, Atom penetrated her, his cock straining, Maia cried out with pleasure. She ran her hands down Atom's back, Dae's chest as he kissed her, enjoying the feel of the two men being so attentive.

She came hard, her head thrown back as Dae sucked on her nipple. Atom bit down on her shoulder then put his lips to her ear. "Touch him, Maia…"

It seemed so natural to slide her hand down to Dae's groin and stroke him until he too was coming, groaning and shuddering.

Maia, her skin on fire, relaxed back as they all caught their breaths. "Wow. Wow. That was incredible."

Atom chuckled. "I couldn't agree more."

"Thirded, if that's a thing."

They all laughed. Dae propped himself up on his elbow. "Thank you for inviting me to join you."

"You invited us, remember?" Maia grinned at him. He really was a sweetheart.

"Oh yes." Dae smiled back at her and Atom. "I have to say, usually my assignations are not as…warm and friendly as this."

Maia touched his face. "I hate to think of you as lonely."

"I'm not, not really. Just sometimes." He looked at Atom. "You have a family?"

"Two kids. Believe it or not, an eighteen-year-old and a seven-year-old."

"Eighteen?" Dae's eyebrows shot up. "No, I don't

believe that." He sighed. "But I'm envious. I'm an only child, and my parents are gone. Believe it or not the entertainment world isn't known for genuine friendships. Not all the time, anyway, some of my clients are good people." He ran his hand through his hair. "So, it's good to know you, even for just one night."

Maia looked at Atom and again, a wordless exchange passed between them. Atom cleared his throat. "You ever get to Seattle, Dae?"

Dae nodded. "I work with Quartet a lot. Tomas Meir is a good friend."

Atom got up and went to his clothes, digging out a business card. "When you're in Seattle, call us. You're welcome whenever."

Dae looked surprised and Maia grinned. "Like you said, we're the friendly type. Come stay with us, if you'd like. Yes?" She looked at Atom who nodded.

"Do. Obviously, this..." Atom indicated the three of them, "would have to stay here and now. But you need friendly faces in Seattle, come see us."

Later, back at the hotel, Atom and Maia lay together in bed, talking about their experience and Dae.

"We got lucky," Maia said, propping her chin on Atom's chest, "he was a sweetheart."

"We did." Atom was tracing his fingers through her hair and Maia studied his eyes.

"Do you have any regrets?"

Atom shook his head. "None… well…"

"What?"

Atom stroked her cheek. "You know… I hope you told him not to penetrate you for your sake, not mine. I said all in, so to speak, and I meant it. What happened in there stays there."

"I said it for me, and for you. The love I have for you. Dae was sexy and sensual and beautiful, yes, but you are the love of my life, Atom Harcourt. I've only been with two men, and I don't count the first." She gave him a half smile. "For me, you are the only one. The only one. I enjoyed tonight, yes, and Dae was perfect but I don't feel the need to repeat it." She grinned suddenly. "Although I ought to repay the favor, I suppose."

Atom's eyes widened. "Wait, you think Beyoncé would be willing?" He grinned as she tickled him. "Look, no, as you say, we've been there, done that. I don't think we'll have any trouble keeping the spark in our sex lives, do you?"

"Not a chance." Maia sat up and straddled him as he smiled up at her. She reached down and stroked his cock between her palms, feeling it twitch and respond. She stroked the tip up and down her wet crease then slowly impaled herself onto it, sighing happily. "Atom?"

"Yes, baby? Oh, that feels so good…" He was distracted and she waited until they had finished making love to finish her thought.

Sated and Atom cradled her in his arms. "What was you going to ask me?"

"I've been thinking lately… um… that maybe, with Luka all grown up, and Eddie in school…"

Atom chuckled. "You want another baby, don't you?"

Maia looked shocked. "You knew?"

"I had an inkling. Just from your little habits when you were pregnant with Eddie. Like dusting more than you usually would, or staring at baby clothes in stores when you think I'm not looking."

Maia made a face at him. "Sneaky."

"Broody."

She chuckled. "I admit I am but, listen, if you're not up for it, I'll get over it. Hormones and all that."
Atom chuckled. "Darling, I always said I wanted a whole bunch of kids with you and I meant it. Let's do it."
"You sure?" Maia traced a line down his chest. "Sure you're just not high after the 'Dae' we've had?"
Atom groaned. "Actually, you're right. If our next child has jokes worse than you, then it would be kindness just to give up now." He kissed her, still laughing. "But really, let's do it. Let's have another kid."

Eighteen months later...

"So, explain this to me. You're not Christians and yet this a kind of Christening?"
Jamelia, having stolen some food from the banquet, was sitting on the kitchen counter as Maia, Emory, Michonne and Unique worked around her. Her mother shot her a warning glance and shooed Jamelia away.
"Think of it more as a naming ceremony and an excuse for a party," Maia said, then her ears pricked up. "Uh-oh, her majesty is bullying her dad again. Excuse me."
She grinned as she took the stairs three at a time and walked into her daughter's bedroom. Luka was giggling at one end of the room, holding her nose as Atom struggled with the apocalypse of his new-born daughter's diaper. Maia couldn't help the laughter when she saw the appalled look on her husband's face.
"It's the worst one yet," he said, weakly. "I'm sure Eddie's were never this bad. It's like she saves them for me."
Maia and Luka were helpless with laughter at the wretched look on his face and he hissed at them. Maia

was unsympathetic. "Listen, I gave birth to her, you can deal with that."

Atom picked up the dirty diaper and threw it into the pail and then chased Maia and Luka around the bedroom with it.

Briar Rose, their three-month-old daughter, watched them, gurgling happily. Atom gave up the chase and returned to his daughter to finish his task. Maia and Luka helped him out then they all went downstairs.

Nella, Emory and Dante's daughter and Luka's girlfriend, greeted them at the bottom of the stairs. "There's a man at the door who, quite frankly, could turn me straight."

Luka snorted and Maia grinned. "That would be Dae."

She went to greet their friend, who looked a bit startled at the amount of people in the house. "Am I too early?"

"Never." Maia hugged him. In the year and a half since their unusual meeting, Dae had become someone who had become very important to their family. He spent a few days here and there with them, but he always kept in touch and when Briar Rose was born, he had sent practically an entire store of clothes and bedding for their daughter.

Both Atom and Maia adored the young man and when he'd told them that he had been hired permanently by Quartet Records and would be based in Seattle for the foreseeable future, they had been delighted. He'd relocated a month ago and Atom had helped him find a home in the city. Surprising them both, he'd been a willing babysitter and Maia wondered if he was ready to start putting down roots, finally.

The Benjamin girls were gaping open mouthed at Dae, who they meeting for the first time and when Lark Sun, Maia's long-time business partner walked in, she joined them in fangirling the beautiful man, here without his otherworldly mask of make-up and contacts and Maia thought he was even more good-looking without them. He did just look like the shy guy from Busan he told them he was.

Before long the party was in full swing, and Maia and Atom conducted a very informal and playful naming ceremony for their daughter, surrounded by love and laughter. Maia got emotional which led to everyone teasing her but she waved away their laughter. "I don't care," she said, "you can all bust my balls, but I'm going to say this. You... my family, my friends, as if there is any difference. Dae, Unique, Jamelia and Michonne... Emory, Dante, Olly... Lark and Nella. We may not be blood relatives but you have given me the family, the big family I never thought I would have. Briar Rose and Eddie, our babies." She giggled as Eddie pulled a sulky face at being called a baby at the big boy age of seven. Maia looked at her eldest daughter, so beautiful, so calm and serene leaning against the wall at the back, her fingers linked with her love's. Luka smiled back at her mother, their bond unbreakable after everything they had been through together. "Luka... our Lulu..." Maia's tears began to fall freely now and Luka chuckled.

"Aw, Mom..."

"Lulu," Maia managed to choke out as the others got teary too. "You are my superheroine, you know that? After everything... you turned out to be just... an angel."

"Hah," said Atom and everyone giggled.

Maia couldn't stop looking at her girl, her Lulu. "Darling, we're so proud of you, and we're so in love that you and Nella have found each other. Me and your Pa," she smiled up at Atom, "we know something about 'meant to be'."

Emory was crying now too as she put her hand on her

own daughter's shoulder. Nella grinned at her. "Mom, really? You two are so mushy, it's disgusting." She was grinning when she said it though, meaning it as a joke and everyone chuckled again.
"I have no shame," Emory shot back with a grin and high-fived Maia, who laughed.
"Nope, nor here. We love you both so much, and we're proud of you for travelling the world and really getting out there. But now, college, right?"
"Right, Mom," Luka shook her head, laughing, "and to make your day, we both decided to apply to UW."
Maia's heart soared and she gasped as the other applauded. "Oh, it's so selfish of me, but thank you."
Luka winked at her and mouthed "I love you, Mom." Maia blew her a kiss.
Then she looked at Atom, her eyes shining. "And you…" She got choked up again and instead pressed her lips to Atom's. The kiss went on and on and Maia heard her friends cheering, but at that moment, no-one existed but him. When they finally broke apart, she stroked his face, her eyes intense on his. "You know," she whispered and he nodded, his own eyes soft with love.
"I know," was all he said but it was everything to her.

It was already after midnight when the final guests drifted away. Emory, Dante, Luka and Nella stayed last and Maia hugged them both as they helped her clean up the kitchen. The two girls kept exchanging giggles and secret glances until finally Emory broke and asked them what they were hiding.
Luka and Nella rounded up their parents and sat them down in the living room. "We have news."
Emory and Maia looked at each other and suddenly knew

exactly what their daughters were about to tell them. They smiled at each other.

It was as they expected—Luka and Nella had decided to marry before they began college together. "We've already talked about getting an apartment together and we thought, why wait? It's not like we're ever going to split."

"Anyone else, I would say that was a foolish thing to say at your age," Dante said, "but not you two."

"Thanks, Dad," Nella hugged her father. "We didn't want to make a huge announcement today, today was about Briar."

"The B-Rose." Luka interjected with a grin, knowing Maia hated the nickname. Maia mock-scowled at her and winked at Nella.

"Good luck with her. She gets her sense of humor from Atom."

"Hey." Atom chuckled. "Dad jokes are the new black."

"Dear god," Nella said with an alarmed look. "Is this my future?"

They all laughed. "Suck it up, ho." Luka said with a fond look at her fiancée. "Come on, we have plenty of time to celebrate. Let's allow these old folks to get their beauty sleep... god knows they need it."

"Any chance you could take her as your lawful wife sooner?" Maia said but laughed, hugging them both. "We'll celebrate properly soon, I promise."

Finally, at nearly two a.m., Maia and Atom checked on their two youngest children, both sleeping soundly, Eddie at a weird angle as always, his feet sticking out of the side of the bed. Maia covered his feet with the blanket and kissed his forehead.

She met Atom coming out of Briar's room. "She

sleeping?"

"Like this?" Atom did an impersonation of his baby daughter, sleeping with all her limbs sticking out and her mouth wide open.

Maia giggled. "Oh, you silly man. Come to bed."

When they had washed up and slipped into bed, Atom wrapped his arms around her. "You sleepy?"

"Yes, but no if you're thinking of giving some of that good loving." Maia wiggled her eyebrows at him and he chuckled.

"Okay, if you insist…" He rolled her onto her back and Maia giggled as he showered kisses down on her face and lips. He moved down, trailing his lips along her jawline, her throat, until he reached her nipples. He took each into his mouth in turn, sucking and teasing them until they were rock-hard and uber-sensitive. Maia stroked her fingers through his dark curls, completely relaxed.

"Are you sure you're not too tired for this?"

Atom grinned up at her. "Could never happen. Just lay back, baby, and let me love you."

Maia sank back onto the pillows as his lips moved softly over her belly and she felt him push her legs apart. He was right, she would never be too tired for his touch, and even after all these years, it still thrilled her even when he looked at her and held her gaze for a beat too long.

She sighed and gasped gently as his tongue twisted around her clit, sending electric sparks of pleasure through her entire being.

Atom slid two fingers into her wet warmth and Maia ground her sex against his hand, getting more excited as he worked, until she just wanted his cock inside her and nothing else.

"Such a greedy, impatient girl," Atom laughed but Maia just moaned at him.

"Put that inside me, Harcourt, right now."

Atom grinned and thrust his straining, thick cock into her, slamming his hips hard and long against her, making her groan and gasp with the force of his lovemaking. Maia couldn't help the huge rush of pleasure erupting inside of her as she came, hard, arching her back up and shivering as she moaned.

"God, Atom... Atom..."

She felt him tense and then tremble as his own peak hit and then they were holding each other and catching their breath. Atom ran his hand down her body, down her curves, tracing a finger on the silvery stretch marks from her pregnancy. "Every inch of you is perfect, you know that, woman?"

Maia giggled and snuggled closer to him. "Even after all these years, I still can't get over the fact that you're mine, that I was lucky enough to tame the wild man."

"Ha, hardly wild, but you had me the moment I saw you out on that balcony."

They gazed at each other for a long time, both lost in recollection of everything they had been through. Atom stroked his fingertip down her cheek, his eyes soft. "It's been quite a ride, hasn't it?"

"It sure has." Maia cupped his face in her hand. "But I love you more than you will ever know, Atom Harcourt."

He smiled. "Trust me..."

"You know?" She was smiling now and he nodded.

"Yes, my darling, my beautiful, wonderful Maia... I know."

And for the rest of the night, he showed her over and over and over again...

The End.

ALL RIGHTS RESERVED. No part of this publication may be reproduced or transmitted in any form whatsoever, electronic, or mechanical, including photocopying, recording, or by any informational storage or retrieval system without express written, dated and signed permission from the author.

DISCLAIMER AND/OR LEGAL NOTICES:
Every effort has been made to accurately represent this book and it's potential. Results vary with every individual, and your results may or may not be different from those depicted. No promises, guarantees or warranties, whether stated or implied, have been made that you will produce any specific result from this book. Your efforts are individual and unique, and may vary from those shown. Your success depends on your efforts, background and motivation.

The material in this publication is provided for educational and informational purposes only and is not intended as medical advice. The information contained in this book should not be used to diagnose or treat any illness, metabolic disorder, disease or health problem. Always consult your physician or health care provider before beginning any nutrition or exercise program. Use of the programs, advice, and information contained in this book is at the sole choice and risk of the reader.

www.ingramcontent.com/pod-product-compliance
Lightning Source LLC
LaVergne TN
LVHW021708060526
838200LV00050B/2563